The CONJURERS

RISE OF THE SHADOW

BRIAN ANDERSON

CROWN BOOKS FOR YOUNG READERS

NEW YORK

Copyright © 2020 by Brian Anderson

All rights reserved. Published in the United States by
Crown Books for Young Readers, an imprint of Random House Children's Books,
a division of Penguin Random House LLC, New York.

Crown and the colophon are registered trademarks of Penguin Random House LLC.

Visit us on the Web! rhcbooks.com

Educators and librarians, for a variety of teaching tools,
visit us at RHTeachersLibrarians.com

Library of Congress Cataloging-in-Publication Data is available upon request.
ISBN 978-0-553-49865-3 (trade) — ISBN 978-0-553-49866-0 (lib. bdg.) —
ISBN 978-0-553-49867-7 (ebook)

Printed in the United States of America
10 9 8 7 6 5 4 3 2 1
First Edition

For Uncle Fred, who taught me my first magic trick and that every person has a story. All you have to do is listen.

CHAPTER 1

ALEX

"Angel Xavier is a fraud," Alex Maskelyne told his older sister, Emma. He barely ducked the pillow she flung at his head. "There's no way the guy is a real magician. He's not even a good stage magician."

Emma seemed about to reach for another pillow but turned back to the TV set instead. Ignoring her brother, she leaned closer to the screen, careful not to disturb the small white rabbit sleeping on her lap.

"Angel used a body double that time he walked through the Great Wall of China," Alex insisted, as though Emma were arguing with him. "And he made the Eiffel Tower vanish by rotating the room where the audience was sitting. Clever camera angles helped, of course. Then when he—"

Emma's hand shot out. The second pillow landed squarely in Alex's face.

"Shut it before Uncle Mordo hears you," Emma ordered him, keeping her own voice low. "I'm trying to watch."

Their uncle forbade television. Since he was their guardian, teacher, and supreme tyrant all in one (at least that was what Alex liked to call him), there was no way to argue or cajole him into buying a TV once he'd decided not to.

So Alex had built the set they were watching from bits and pieces he'd found in the trash or tucked away in the attic of their uncle's Victorian mansion.

Alex hadn't dared hide the TV in his bedroom or in Emma's. Uncle Mordo would have been sure

to find it. But this room, tucked away on the fourth floor of the west wing, was likely safe. It was a small, bare space with a slanted ceiling and a single window, probably a servant's bedroom once upon a time. Uncle Mordo would never come up here.

On the TV screen, Angel Xavier stood with one foot on either side of a set of railroad tracks. His wrists and ankles had been shackled to posts. He yanked at the chains with all his might, but they held firm.

Suddenly a woman's angular face filled the screen. "Welcome back to *Faster than a Speeding Bullet*! We're offering live coverage of Angel Xavier's greatest escape attempt." She held a microphone with one gloved hand, gesturing toward the tracks behind her with the other. "Hear that? That is the whistle of the train merely seconds away. Angel Xavier has yet to free himself from any of his restraints."

The screen flashed, filling with static.

"Hey! What happened?" Emma jolted upright, waking the rabbit napping on her lap. It jumped from her arms. "Sorry, Pimawa. Alex, you said you fixed it! I'm going to miss Angel's escape!"

"Relax." Her brother slipped out of his chair. He went behind the television and adjusted the cluster of wires and rods sprouting from its case. "I did fix it and . . ." He twisted a wire around a copper tube. The screen flashed back to life. "There. I've fixed it again."

"What's that?" The reporter's voice crackled through the duct tape that held the speakers together. "We're getting word that there appears to be a problem. Of course, it's all part of the drama, folks." She managed a nervous smile. "Over there you can see the emergency crews standing by. Um, again, I'm sure this is all part of the show. . . ."

The camera zoomed in on Angel's horror-stricken face. Veins in his forehead bulged from the effort to free himself. The camera pulled back as the train raced down the track, twenty tons of steel closing in on the magician.

"Oh no! No! No! Can the train stop in time?" the reporter gasped.

The train locked its brakes. Sparks erupted from underneath its metal belly.

Angel Xavier screamed. Emma nearly did too.

Then a strange blue light engulfed the magician. A second later, the screeching train barreled over the spot where he'd stood. The emergency crews rushed onto the tracks as the light faded, but Angel Xavier was gone.

The camera panned the anxious crowd. Everyone was watching and waiting for the magician to make his reappearance. They were still waiting when the screen fizzled and went black.

"Not again!" Emma sprang out of her chair. "I'll miss the best part!"

"The best part? Emma, it's all a stunt, remember?" Alex stood, stretched, and headed for the door.

Emma blocked his path. "Our deal is off. I didn't get to see the end."

"C'mon, Em." Alex groaned. "You don't have to see the end to know it's only a trick. They pumped that blue fog out of hidden pipes and he dropped into a secret dugout next to the tracks. They'll let the audience freak out for a bit; then Angel Xavier will pop up behind the crowd."

"You are so boring." Emma rolled her eyes. "Can't you enjoy anything without picking it apart?"

Alex looked genuinely confused. "What's the fun in that?"

"I'm still not doing your chores."

"No way, Em, we agreed. You got to watch your show, so now you get to do the laundry for a week. A deal's a deal."

"I didn't get to watch *all* my show. Keep your voice down. Uncle Mordo will hear you," said Emma.

"Keep *your* voice down."

"Or maybe we *should* get caught," said Emma. "That'll teach you to break a deal."

"I'm not the one who broke the——" Alex's voice choked off as a large shadow filled the doorway behind him. Cringing, he turned to face the stern eyes of the supreme tyrant—Uncle Mordo.

"One week's banishment from the library for you, Master Maskelyne, except for classes," said Uncle Mordo. He clasped his hands behind his back. His black-and-gold kimono swung around his ankles. "As for you, Miss Maskelyne, you shall polish the entire Victrola collection. To your rooms! Both of you."

It was a trek from the fourth floor of the west wing to their rooms on the third floor of the east wing.

"This is all your fault," Alex grumbled, stomping down the iron spiral staircase.

"You were perfectly happy about it when you thought it would get you out of doing the laundry," Emma snapped back. "Did Uncle Mordo seem kind of . . . weird to you?"

"Dictators are always weird," said Alex. "No library for a week! No fair!"

They had reached the bottom of the landing and were headed along the hallway toward their rooms.

"He seemed distracted," said Emma thoughtfully. "Honestly, I thought he'd be a lot madder."

"Well, you enjoy your lucky break while wiping down hundred-year-old record players," said Alex. "I've had enough of Uncle Mordo and all his rules."

"This again?" said Emma. "We are not running away."

"Of course we're not." Alex grinned. "We're escaping."

Emma pulled ahead, her mouth shut tight.

"It's really simple," Alex huffed behind her. "I have it mapped out. The security system is a joke. We can be over the wall in two minutes thirty-nine seconds. I've been training for weeks, pretending I'm bird-watching."

"And where would we go once we're over the wall?" Emma asked icily.

"Derren Fallow. We find Derren." Alex smirked. That was his trump card. He knew how much his sister liked Derren.

It was very odd that Derren and Mordo were such old friends, when they were nothing alike, nothing at all. Derren told jokes; Uncle Mordo gave orders. Derren brought gifts; Uncle Mordo gave homework assignments. On his last visit Derren had given Alex a ratchet set, which had come in very handy for fixing up the TV. Emma had gotten a horde of orc figurines. She had them tucked away in all sorts of odd places around her bedroom.

But Emma did not seem to be reacting as positively to this part of the plan as Alex had thought she would. "Your plan is to run away to Derren Fallow?" she asked skeptically.

"Exactly," Alex said. He slipped ahead of Emma and wedged himself between her and the door to her room.

"It'll never work. He'll bring us right back to Uncle Mordo."

"No. He won't," Alex said. "Derren knows what it's like here. Come on, Em. You know this is crazy. We're trapped like prisoners. We can only go out if Uncle Mordo goes with us. We don't even get to go to school like normal kids! We've got to escape somehow."

"Alex, we can't leave. Not until Mom and Dad come and get us, any day now."

Alex shook his head. "They're not coming, Em. Please. They're *dead*."

Emma's eyes grew wide and shocked, almost as if her brother had hit her. Then they narrowed. Her lower lip, which had begun to quiver, set in a hard line.

"That's *not* true," said Emma, shoving her brother out of her way.

She entered her room and slammed the door behind her.

EMMA

Emma carefully stepped around her army—tin soldiers, orc figurines, china dolls, and one taxidermied squirrel. Before

heading upstairs to watch TV with Alex, she had led them into battle against the evil cymbal-playing monkey that reigned from atop her pillow.

Emma eyed the books on the shelves that lined her walls. Normally, when she was upset—when she'd had a fight with Alex or gotten in trouble with Uncle Mordo—those books were her comfort. Alex was always talking about escaping, but Emma had her escape right here. Just flip open a few pages and she could be creeping through the forests of Mirkwood or strolling through the snowy woods of Narnia, arm in arm with a faun who'd invited her to tea. She could be soaring over the seas on dragonback or studying her arithmancy lessons in her tower dormitory.

But for once, Emma didn't feel like reading. She swatted

the monkey aside, knelt, and pulled something out from under the bed.

A suitcase. Carefully, Emma brushed every speck of dust off the top of the case. Then she unzipped it to check on everything inside.

Jeans. T-shirts. A dress and a sweater. A pair of sneakers. Socks and underwear. Everything neatly folded, everything ready to go.

Just as soon as her parents came back.

That would show Alex. That would show everyone. They'd see that Emma was the one who'd never lost faith. Who'd always believed that they were coming back.

Soon. Soon. *Soon.*

ALEX

There were two hundred and fifty-two rooms in the mansion. Alex didn't care about any of them.

Except one. The library.

Books were the only proof Alex had that the world outside his uncle's mansion was really there. A normal world, where people studied electronics and learned to program computers and even went to college to be engineers instead of getting homeschooled by an uncle and writing essays about the six wives of King Henry the Eighth. Or was it the eight wives of King Henry the Sixth? Alex could never remember.

And now he was banned from the library for a week. A week!

For doing what? Watching a television show. One that millions of other people were probably watching right now.

Completely, utterly, unbelievably unfair.

Inside his own room, Alex dropped onto the rickety stool in front of his drafting table. His mechanical dog, Bartleby, stood watchfully at the top of his desk, his metal tail alert. Underneath Bartleby was the plan Alex had drawn for the TV set.

It worked. Just like Bartleby worked. Just like nothing else about Alex's life had worked since his parents had left him and his sister with Uncle Mordo while they went on an archaeological dig, only to never come back.

There had been some kind of accident at the dig site. Alex didn't know the details. Uncle Mordo had never volunteered them, and Alex had never asked. He'd been two years old when it happened. And even now, eight years later, Emma was still living in some kind of a dream world where Mom and Dad would show up at the front door. At thirteen, Emma should've known better.

Alex certainly did. Alex faced facts. Angel Xavier was nothing but a stupid show-off, Uncle Mordo was a dictator, and his parents weren't coming back. Ever.

Alex took a pocket watch from his cargo pants, carefully tracing the initials—*H.M.*—engraved on the cover before flipping it open. *H* for Henry—Alex's father's name. *M* for Maskelyne.

The watch was the only thing Alex owned that had once belonged to his father. Its hands were forever frozen at a quarter past three. Alex could fix almost anything, but he'd never fixed this watch. He didn't want to. Somehow, the broken watch made him feel just a bit closer to the parents he could not even remember.

"Hey, Bartleby," said Alex with a sigh, tucking the watch back into his pocket. "Even without legs, you still had a better day than me." He cranked the knob on Bartleby's toaster head.

The mechanical dog sprang to life, cocking his head side to side on noisy gears. A tongue made from a barber's razor strop lolled from his mouth. Alex tossed him a small bolt, which the dog snapped out of the air. He grinned when he heard it rattling around inside Bartleby's copper belly.

From under the ink blotter, Alex pulled out a series of hand-drawn maps. He studied the top one: a floor plan of the mansion with a route highlighted in yellow.

"We'll get out of here, Bartleby. I promise." He scratched Bartleby's leather ears and set the dog's tail wagging.

"The hardest part is going to be convincing Emma." Alex sighed again. It was tempting to just take off by himself, but his sister was all the family he had left. (Uncle Mordo, obviously, didn't count.)

He'd figure it out. One day he'd find a way to get Emma to face reality. Then the two of them would be gone.

Alex figured that Emma would probably be ready to listen to reason once she was done cleaning all seventeen of Uncle Mordo's antique Victrolas.

As Alex rolled up the maps and carefully placed them into a backpack stuffed with tools and rope, an arc of yellow light swung over his desk, glinting off Bartleby's chrome head. A car's headlight? Alex climbed onto his desk and looked out the window.

The only visitors they ever got were Uncle Mordo's fellow antiques dealers. As far as Alex was concerned, they were as dull as the rusty drainpipe outside the window. Except for Derren Fallow, of course.

But the other dealers always arrived one at a time. And they never came at night. Now a group of three was getting out of the car together and striding through the dark toward the veranda that led to the mansion's front door.

As Alex's favorite detective, Sherlock Holmes, would have put it, "The game's afoot!"

"Whoa, Bartleby," Alex muttered. "What's going on? There's Mary McDurphy. You remember her. She gives me itchy sweaters on my birthday every year. At least Derren's here. Boy, he doesn't look thrilled." When the group of visitors came into range of the light near the front door, Alex understood why. Derren was walking next to Christopher Agglar. "He's the worst of the whole bunch," Alex told Bartleby. "The only man Uncle Mordo could beat in a personality contest."

The newcomers crowded onto the veranda and were lost to Alex's view. A moment later, Alex heard the front door of the house open and close.

He climbed off the desk and flopped back onto his stool. "Bartleby, what are they doing here this late?" he asked.

Bartleby looked back at him with a knowing expression in his beady black eyes.

"None of my business, huh? I should go to bed. Not worry about what they're up to. Because if Uncle Mordo

catches me snooping around, I'll get into a ton of trouble. That's what you're trying to tell me?"

Alex reached out and tapped Bartleby on the head, making the little dog nod.

"But I'm *already* in trouble," Alex pointed out. "So what's a little more?"

CHAPTER 2

ALEX

Alex hugged the wall as he headed down the main staircase. He'd gotten out of his room and to the second floor without encountering a soul. But once he reached the first floor, the riskiest part of his mission would begin.

Luckily, Uncle Mordo's study was only a few steps from the bottom of the staircase. Alex took those steps as stealthily as possible. His sneakers made no noise at all on the shiny, slippery marble floor.

The doors to Uncle Mordo's study were closed. Alex pulled a stethoscope from his sweatshirt pocket and placed the chest piece against the polished oak.

At first all he heard was hushed, garbled conversation. It was like listening to a television through a seashell. Alex began to fear that his daring escapade was nothing but a waste of time. After all, what could he possibly hope to hear? A bunch of eccentrics complaining that people were finally tired of buying old, broken stuff?

It wasn't worth the risk after all. Alex was about to pocket his stethoscope and retreat upstairs when Agglar's voice rose above the rest.

"Yes, I am certain. The Shadow Conjurer is behind Angel Xavier's disappearance. It is time to act. It is our duty to protect the Conjurian. I am calling for even stronger measures to—"

"Do you think he will come after the children?" asked a woman's voice. Mary McDurphy.

Perhaps the group inside had moved closer to the door, because now Alex could hear them quite clearly.

"The Maskelynes were clever magicians," said Agglar. "Henry and Evelynne perfected the elephant-teleportation illusion in their stage act."

"And what does elephant teleportation have to do with the problem we are facing?" snapped Derren Fallow.

"I mention elephant teleportation," Agglar said icily, "merely to point out that it would have been a simple feat for the Maskelynes to hide the Eye before they perished. Unfortunately, they seem to have hidden it so well that no one has yet been able to find it. Therefore our foe will pursue every avenue that might yield a clue to its whereabouts. That includes the children."

"He can try," Alex heard his uncle say. "He won't succeed. The security systems here would baffle Houdini."

Deeply confused, Alex pressed the stethoscope deeper into his ears. Magicians? The Conjurian? Elephants? What were they talking about?

The best thing to do, he decided, would be to gather as much information as he could, then process it once he was safely back in his room. That was the plan right up until a hand clamped onto his shoulder and he fell on his butt, dropping his stethoscope onto the floor.

"What are you doing?" Emma whispered. She was wearing a long belted pink sweater with her favorite T-shirt and leggings underneath. Her rabbit was squirming in her arms.

"What are *you* doing?" hissed Alex.

"Pimawa got out of my room. I had to catch him. Hurry, we'd better get back before Uncle Mordo finds out."

On the other side of the study door, someone shouted angrily. Alex grabbed his stethoscope, scrambling to his feet. "We have to hide! Quick!"

He dragged his sister across the foyer. Next to the staircase, a suit of samurai armor stood at attention. Alex pulled Emma down behind it as the study door burst open.

Derren Fallow stormed into the hallway.

"We are not finished," Agglar called out, following right behind.

"We *are* finished. Our world is dying, Christopher. Magic is dying. And what do we do?" Derren snatched his wool jacket off the coat rack beside the front door. "Hide in our tower? Our people need us. It's time for action, not more talking!"

"Your idealistic youth has blinded you to the real threat!" shouted Agglar. The wrinkles on his face tightened, like cracks in cement.

"I think I know what the real threat is," Derren said coldly. He slung his jacket on and yanked on his hat.

Uncle Mordo walked out of the study as well, his kimono swirling. He stepped between his two friends. "Let us keep this civil," he said, frowning. "And quiet."

"The children deserve to know the truth," Derren snapped. "They have to, if they're going to survive."

Emma, wide-eyed, met Alex's gaze. He saw that his sister was frightened.

He was too, but he put his finger to his lips. They had to find out what was going on. Staying unnoticed was their best bet.

Agglar ignored Uncle Mordo, glowering at Derren. "If you leave now," he said with a threat in his voice, "you are banished from the Circle."

Derren did not even answer. He gave Mordo a curt nod, turned up his jacket collar, and left.

Agglar and Mordo stood staring after him. Then Uncle Mordo shook his head.

"He will come around," said Mordo. Putting a hand on

Agglar's arm, he guided the other man back toward the study. "We still have much to discuss."

Agglar pulled away. "No," he said, grabbing his hat and cane from the rack. "Master Fallow was correct on one point. The time for talk is over. I must return to the Conjurian at once."

Emma's brow furrowed. "The Conjurian?" she breathed.

Alex scowled at her and shook his head very slightly. They couldn't afford to make any noise.

"Be safe, my friend," said Agglar, and walked onto the porch. Dead leaves blew inside and rattled over the marble floor as the doors closed behind him.

Pimawa twitched in Emma's arms. Emma looked as if she wanted to squirm as well, but she held still at Alex's side as Uncle Mordo headed back to the study.

Alex let out a slow breath. Mordo didn't know that he and Emma were hidden here, that they'd heard the entire bizarre conversation. He'd reenter the study, and Alex and Emma would head back upstairs to figure out what was going on.

But at the study door, Mordo paused. He turned slowly, frowning. His eyes swept the hall. Then he walked, step by deliberate step, toward the stairway and the suit of armor standing at its foot.

Emma's face twisted with worry. She hugged Pimawa close.

Mordo paused not three steps away from the spot where his niece and nephew huddled in their hiding place. He seemed almost to be listening to something. Alex knew what was going on. His uncle would wait until either he or Emma could not stand it anymore. He'd wait until they crawled out, ashamed, begging for forgiveness.

Well, it wasn't going to happen like that.

Alex crawled out, all right, but he wasn't begging for forgiveness. He wasn't begging for anything. Once he got clear of the statue, he jumped to his feet, ready to burst out with all the questions crowding his mind.

Why had Derren and Agglar been talking about his parents? What was the Conjurian? What was the Circle? Why had everybody been so angry?

Alex met Uncle Mordo's furious gaze with his own equally angry one. But to his surprise, Mordo wasn't looking at Alex. The man was looking over the boy's head at the staircase that rose into the gloom of the second floor.

Emma squirmed out from behind the statue and got awkwardly to her feet, clinging to Pimawa. The rabbit struggled in her arms as if he wanted to leap out and run far away.

"What's going on?" Emma asked uncertainly. Pimawa lunged and she gripped him harder.

"Run!" yelled Uncle Mordo.

Alex turned and looked up to see what had caught his uncle's attention. He wasn't even frightened by what he saw on the staircase, because he was quite sure that it couldn't possibly be real.

Moon-white skulls missing their bottom jaws emerged from a swirling mass of tattered black cloth. There were five or six of the creatures clustered at the top of the stairs. Their eyeless sockets seemed to be looking directly at Alex and his sister.

Uncle Mordo stepped in front of Alex and Emma, between them and the strange creatures, which had started to drift slowly down the staircase. "Mary! Rag-O-Rocs!" he shouted. "We need you!"

A huge noise, as if a truck had slammed into the front of the house, assaulted Alex's eardrums. When he spun around, he saw that the front doors had been blasted off their hinges. The doors hit the marble tiles of the hallway, revealing another black-robed figure standing on the doorstep.

It wasn't quite the same as the things on the stairs, though. This monster had a face, not just a fleshless skull. It was a sickly blue, marked by three red scars that ran from forehead to chin.

But just like the staircase fiends—what had Uncle Mordo called them? Rag-O-Rocs?—this thing's eyeless face seemed to be staring eagerly, hungrily, at Alex and Emma.

Not two seconds had gone by since Alex had looked up the stairs to see something that couldn't possibly be there. He grabbed Emma's arm, trying to protect her and keep her close. What should they do? Should they run? Should they laugh? Surely this was just some kind of trick. A crazy joke. A Halloween prank come early.

"Mordo?" Mary McDurphy poked her head outside the study door. "What on earth is—the Shadow Conjurer! He's here!" She charged toward the doorway, purple umbrella leveled at the intruder. "Get the children out!"

The creature in the doorway—Alex guessed that the thing was called the Shadow Conjurer—twitched his veiny hand. A blur of black cloth and bone shot out into the hallway and swept Mary McDurphy back into the study. Awful yells and clattering came from inside.

Alex was beginning to realize that, whatever was happening, it was no game, or joke, or trick. It was serious.

Deadly serious.

The figure with the scarred face stepped into the foyer. Behind him, a wall of his skeletal minions in their floating black robes blocked the entrance.

"I must say," said the man Mary McDurphy had called the Shadow Conjurer, "this was quite gracious of you, Mordo.

Gathering the Circle members and the Maskelyne children together for me."

Alex, still holding on to Emma's arm, was finally ready to obey his uncle's orders and run—but where? Those creepy Rag-O-Rocs were on the staircase, and the Shadow Conjurer was blocking the door. Into the study? But that was a dead end. There'd be no way out.

From behind, Mordo's arms came around Alex and Emma in a tight hug.

He bent low so that they could hear his whispered words.

"I'm so sorry. I have failed you and your parents," he said. "Now you must do exactly as I tell you. Follow Pimawa. Do you understand? No matter what, follow Pimawa."

He kissed each of them firmly on top of the head. "I love you both. I am truly sorry."

Then Mordo whipped off his kimono and draped it over the children like a tent.

A thin layer of black-and-gold silk could be no protection at all against floating skeletons or a scarred man with a dreadful eyeless face. Alex was ready to fling the cloth aside, to fight, or at least to run. Anything was better than huddling under a robe, unable to see, unable to escape—

Then the floor gave way underneath Alex and his sister. They were falling.

EMMA

Emma hit the library floor hard, with Alex right behind her. Pimawa landed lightly beside them, then used Alex's head as a trampoline to bound over both brother and sister, heading for the far end of the long room with its rows of bookshelves.

"Ow!" said Alex, rubbing his rear end. Emma just sat, watching the wall panel slide back over the secret passage that had swept them away from the front hall. They'd slid down a slick metal ramp and ended up here, in the narrow room lined with Uncle Mordo's bookshelves and cabinets. Seventeen antique Victrolas had been arranged artfully against one wall.

"What were those things?" Emma asked. Cold shivers had taken hold of her from deep inside, and she felt as if she'd never be warm again. "That man, he didn't have—" She shuddered. "He didn't have eyes."

Boom! It sounded as if a boulder had hit the library doors.

She looked at Alex. Alex was the logical one. Alex always had a plan. Surely Alex would know what to do now.

He didn't disappoint her. "I think, for now," her brother said, helping Emma to her feet, "we should get as far away from those doors as possible."

Bam! The doors began to splinter.

They raced down the long library floor. At the far end, they found Pimawa clambering up a statue of the caterpillar from *Alice in Wonderland*. It was Emma's favorite. Alex would always complain that a story filled with illogical gibberish should have no place in a library, but Emma loved the dream-like madness of the tale—Alice growing and shrinking, the tea party shifting seats every minute, the Queen of Hearts shrieking, "Off with their heads!"

She thought she might love it less after tonight.

Pimawa crouched and hammered the caterpillar's hookah with his back legs. The statue creaked, deep inside. Then, to Emma's shock, it split in two. The halves swung apart, like a set of doors on hinges, to reveal—another secret passage?

Not quite. A secret staircase.

A spiral staircase, made of wrought iron, descended into the floor from the space formerly occupied by the statue. Pimawa dove down the steps.

"You've got to be kidding me," Alex said, shaking his head.

"Come on!" Emma pulled at his sleeve.

"But where does that staircase go? We can't just—"

Bang! Crack!

That, Emma thought, was probably the sound of the library doors splitting apart.

"Uncle Mordo told us to follow Pimawa!" she shouted at Alex. "We have to trust him! Come on!"

"Are you telling me to trust Uncle Mordo? Or a rabbit?" Alex demanded. But as Emma darted down the steps, he followed her.

Behind them, the library doors imploded in a shower of timber and metal. The siblings were more than halfway down the winding steps when an unearthly cry echoed above them.

Emma leaped off the last step, and her feet thumped on hard-packed earth. Alex landed behind her and grabbed at her hand. A narrow passageway stretched before them, with walls and a roof of stone and a floor of dirt. Emma could glimpse Pimawa's small white form several yards ahead.

The passageway twisted and turned, and Alex and Emma followed it, with Pimawa leading the way. They skidded around one final corner and saw that the tunnel stretched another twenty feet or so in front of them and then came to an abrupt end.

At the end of the passageway, a small red box sat on a narrow black pedestal. Pimawa crouched on top of the box, gnawing the latch on the front.

Alex groaned.

"This is where the stupid rabbit led us?" he asked in disbelief. "A dead end? Come on. Let's go back. We've got to find another way out."

"No. We're supposed to follow Pimawa, remember," Emma reminded him. Uncle Mordo had been trying to protect them; she knew it. He would not have told them to follow the rabbit without a good reason.

"Not if Pimawa wants to get devoured by a demonic skeleton!" Alex yanked on Emma's sweater.

Emma shook him off impatiently. She was studying Pimawa, who was still gnawing at the box's latch. "No, Alex, look. He wants us to open it."

"It's probably filled with moldy carrots," Alex growled. "Emma! Get real! This is serious! Come with me!"

Still facing Emma, he took a step along the way they had come. The walls shook.

Alex looked over his shoulder and yelped. Emma did the same and bit back a shriek. The ivory skull shrouded by tattered cloth hissed as it came around the corner.

Alex spun to face the monster. "Stay close to me, Emma!" he yelled. "Get ready to run!"

Emma shook her head. She stepped away from Alex, nearer the box on its pedestal. She grabbed Pimawa and held him tightly.

The Rag-O-Roc drifted closer. It seemed in no hurry, as if it knew they could not get away.

Emma flipped open the lid of the box.

Something inside unleashed a cloud of swirling blue light. Pimawa leaped out of Emma's arms, straight into the light, and vanished.

Deep down, Emma knew what to do.

"Alex! Follow the rabbit!" Emma shouted. "We have to follow Pimawa!"

She stuck her hand into the light.

It warmed her arm from the inside out, slowly spreading through her body. The light tugged at her—gently, at first. Then she plunged down a waterfall of light, wondering when she would crash into solid ground, or if she would land at all.

CHAPTER 3

ALEX

"Emma!" Alex shouted as loud as he could. But the thick fog all around him choked off his shouts.

He didn't know where he was or how he'd gotten here. That terrifying skeleton monster had been stalking him down the tunnel, and he'd been backing away, expecting to bump into Emma at any second. Emma had yelled something crazy about her rabbit, and then—whoosh! It had been like he'd slipped onto a waterslide, except it was a waterslide made out of warm blue light.

And when he was done sliding, he was here. Wherever here was.

"Emma!" he yelled again.

The fog was so thick that he could barely see his own hands. He *couldn't* see his feet. There might be a cliff three feet ahead of him, and he wouldn't know about it until he was falling.

"Think," Alex told himself. "Think! That's your only chance."

He stood still and thought.

"Okay. Yelling isn't working," he told himself, talking out loud because it felt a bit comforting to hear his own voice. "I could walk right past Emma and never know it. The logical thing to do is stay put. Wait for this fog to clear."

Okay. That was what he'd do. Stay put.

He sat. The damp cold seeped through his pants, which did nothing to make him feel better. He focused on his breathing, calling out for his sister after every tenth breath. But she never answered. Or maybe she was shouting his name somewhere close by, and he just couldn't hear her. The clinging, sticky fog swallowed every sound.

And that was why Alex never heard the leviathan until it emerged from the swirling mist inches from his face.

Okay. This was obviously a hallucination. Alex had heard

that if people stayed in complete darkness for long enough, they started to see made-up things floating all around them. Staring at blank gray mist probably did exactly the same thing.

Nevertheless, Alex scuttled backward like a crab on his hands and feet. And bumped into something furry and warm.

Soft paws grabbed hold of him. Alex twisted around, coming face to face with a furry monster with long ears and a twitching pink nose. He would have screamed except for the fact that the creature was wearing his sister's sweater.

If this was a hallucination, it certainly had some odd details. . . .

"It's okay, Alex" came a voice out of the mist.

Emma appeared at the creature's side, smiling reassuringly.

"It's only Pimawa," she told him.

Only Pimawa. Of course it was. How silly of him. Rabbits generally grew to the size of ten-year-old boys, walked on their hind legs, and addressed him as . . .

"Master Alex, please pardon my current state of attire," said Pimawa, pulling the sweater closed over his thick white fur. "I understand much of this is quite overwhelming. However, we do not, in the present environment, have time for lengthy explanations."

Alex's jaw opened and closed without making a sound.

"Master Alex?" the rabbit repeated. He looked concerned. His ears twitched.

Emma lightly punched Alex's shoulder. "Don't worry. Pimawa's cool. I mean he was awesome before, but look. Now he's *really* awesome!"

Pimawa waved one paw, as if embarrassed by the praise. "Down to business," he said.

"Hang on a second," said Alex. He raised his voice a little. "What's going *on*?"

A furry white finger pressed against Alex's lips.

"We've escaped the Shadow Conjurer for now, but he's still chasing the Eye of Dedi," Pimawa said in a low voice. "I'll explain everything about the Conjurian later. Right now I'm under strict orders from your uncle, and the first priority is to get both of you someplace safe. Follow me!" Pimawa took off at a quick pace on his gigantic white feet.

"Follow the rabbit, Alex," Emma said with a grin. A grin! The world had turned upside down, nothing made any sense, and she was grinning! Plus, she wanted them both to follow a talking rabbit! Did she think she was Alice in Wonderland?

Emma grabbed Alex's sweatshirt and pulled him along after Pimawa. Alex only let himself be dragged because he couldn't think of anything else to do. He could glimpse the rabbit's furry back and the fluttering of Emma's pink sweater a few feet ahead. Pimawa led them up and over a rocky slope. As the ground flattened out, he stopped, lifting a paw to caution them.

"No sudden movements," Pimawa whispered.

Alex gasped.

There were swirls and flickers in the mist ahead of Pimawa. Alex struggled to focus his eyes and realized he was seeing more giant fish, just like the one that had startled him earlier. They drifted and darted through the fog as if it were water, and Pimawa carefully crept closer to the nearest one.

The fish eyed him doubtfully and seemed about to dash away into the mist. But when Pimawa reached out a gentle paw and began to stroke the fish's silvery scales, just above the fluttering gills, it relaxed. Its fins drooped, and it inched closer and closer to the ground.

"Once they know you mean them no harm, Myst fish are as docile as lambs," Pimawa said.

Emma edged up next to Pimawa and reached out to pet the fish as well. Alex hung back. The animal might have looked peaceful, but it was also huge. It could bite off an arm with one quick snap if it wanted to.

Emma didn't seem to have thought of that. She never *did*

think logically. "What's a Myst fish?" she asked.

"One of a plethora of creatures that live in the Mysts," said Pimawa. "Also, our ride out of here."

"We're going to ride *that*?" Alex did not move closer.

"Yes, and the sooner the better." Pimawa cupped his paws together and nodded at Emma. She stepped onto his paws, and he boosted her up onto the hovering fish. "Your turn, Master Alex. Kindly hurry. Remember what may be pursuing us."

Alex shook his head.

"I already figured it out," he told Pimawa. "We're hallucinating. That's what this is. Moldy flour in our pancakes or something like that. I just have to wait it out, and I'll wake up. Soon."

Something off in the fog howled. Pimawa's ears twisted, homing in on the sound.

"On the fish, now!" he ordered. "If you please."

A second howl sounded closer. Alex was pretty sure you couldn't get hurt in a hallucination. Still . . .

"Now!" Pimawa ordered.

Alex closed the few feet between them, put his foot onto Pimawa's paws, and jumped. Emma grabbed one of his wrists and hauled him up the slippery side of the fish. Alex was pleased to discover that the thing smelled of wet moss as opposed to, well, a giant fish.

Pimawa sprung up in a single bound. Once the three of them were astride the Myst fish, with Pimawa in front, Emma behind, and Alex squashed in the middle, the rabbit showed

them how to grasp the fish's knobby spine and lean forward to maintain balance. Then he slapped the creature's side, sending it swishing off into the gray air.

"Your name is Fornesworth?" asked Alex a short time later.

"Yes," said Pimawa. "Pimawa Fornesworth, at your eternal service."

"So, you're like . . . Uncle Mordo's butler?" asked Alex. This hallucination was certainly complicated.

"May he rest gloriously on the Isle of Dedi," said Pimawa, closing his eyes for a brief moment.

"Wait," Emma broke in. She twisted around to look at Pimawa. "May he rest gloriously? Is that like . . . rest in peace?"

Pimawa nodded. It was hard to see how a rabbit's face could look grief-stricken, but Pimawa's certainly did.

Alex felt his stomach lurch, and not because the fish had taken a sudden dart to the right to go around a mossy hillside. "You mean Uncle Mordo is . . ."

"Your uncle would not have entrusted you to my care if there were any chance he would stay alive to watch over you himself," Pimawa said. "No. He sacrificed himself to slow the Rag-O-Rocs down, giving us all the chance to escape from . . ." His voice grew quiet and apprehensive. "The Shadow Conjurer."

"Oh," Emma said in a small voice. She faced forward once more to stare at the mist surrounding them. Her face was hidden from Alex, but he could tell that tears were slipping down her cheeks.

Alex felt his stomach churn with confusion. Uncle Mordo, the tyrant. The dictator. The man whose rules and orders had driven Alex crazy for years. This was the same man who'd died trying to save Alex and his sister from monsters?

Good thing this was a hallucination or some kind of wild dream. Otherwise, that would be a really horrible thought.

Pimawa glanced at both children and then continued talking.

"And that is as he would have wished it," the rabbit said gently. "As for me . . . butler, no. I am a Jimjarian. We were created to serve magicians. At least those of us fortunate enough to be chosen. And I," continued Pimawa, puffing his chest out, "was chosen by Mordo the Mystifier."

"Mordo the Mystifier?" Alex repeated. He still felt horrible at the idea that Uncle Mordo was . . . dead? Could that actually be true? But he could not stifle a disgraceful urge to laugh. "Sorry. It's just hard to picture Uncle Mordo as a magician. Or doing anything remotely entertaining."

Pimawa patted the fish's head. "Good boy. Straight on for a bit and you shall be free to go about your business." He leaned close to both the children, waving his paws with a dramatic flourish. "*Entertaining?* Master Alex, you do not understand. Your Uncle Mordo could steal thoughts from your head as easily as plucking cotton candy from a paper cone. He made giraffes vanish for kings, walked through walls for emperors, and levitated diplomats."

"Wait. What?" Alex said. "Uncle Mordo did magic tricks for kings and emperors?"

"Not magic *tricks*, Alex," Emma said impatiently. "Don't you get it? He did *real* magic. Magic is real!"

Alex stared at the back of Emma's head in alarm. His sister clearly thought she'd walked into the pages of one of her beloved fantasy novels. He had to bring her back to reality, and fast.

"Emma," he said as patiently as he could, "things are weird, sure, but you know that *magic isn't real.*"

"Alex," she said, echoing his tone of strained patience, "you are riding a giant floating fish."

Pimawa cleared his throat.

"Miss Emma is quite correct, Master Alex. And your uncle's abilities were extraordinary. For these days, at least. In the past, they say, many magicians had far greater powers—but not now."

"Why not?" Emma asked.

Pimawa went on as though he had not heard her. "As for your parents, well, in my humble opinion, *their* magic show was truly special. The love they had for each other—the audience felt it. Every time they produced a dove, or materialized a tiger from thin air, or escaped from a burning stake, they were performing for each other as much as they were for the paying customers."

"What are you talking about?" Alex asked, bewildered. "Our parents were archaeologists, not magicians."

"They were archaeologists, and magicians as well," said Pimawa. "That is why Master Agglar recruited them for MAGE."

"What does that mean?" Emma asked.

"Magic Antiquities Guardianship and Enforcement," Pimawa answered. "Bit of a mouthful. Your parents traveled the world, dazzling audiences with their magic. One time, I remember, they made the crown jewels of England vanish. Caused quite the ruckus until they returned the priceless gems to the Tower of London. But everywhere they ventured, they were secretly recovering lost Conjurian artifacts."

"*What* kind of artifacts?" Alex asked. He was starting to feel dizzy. Every answer Pimawa offered seemed to simply add a new layer of confusion. *Maybe I should stop expecting a hallucination to make sense.*

"Many kinds. But the one they were searching for most assiduously was, of course, the Eye of Dedi."

"What the heck is that?" Alex asked.

Pimawa sighed and shook his head. "There is so much you do not know, Master Alex! How am I ever to explain it all? Every child here in the Conjurian knows the tale of Dedi and his Eye."

"Well, we don't," Alex said impatiently. "So tell us."

"The entire tale? Time is short. For now I will simply say

that it was the Eye of Dedi that created this world. The Conjurian. The world of magicians."

Alex shook his head. "This is another world?"

"Surely, you did not think, Master Alex," Pimawa said patiently, "that we were simply in, say, Omaha, did you? Or Tamil Nadu? Or Antarctica? Look around you."

"Obviously this is a different world, Alex," Emma chimed in.

"Probably I've just gone insane," Alex said irritably.

"Well, I haven't," Emma snapped. "And I want to hear Pimawa explain things. So stop interrupting him. Were our mom and dad looking for that Eye of Dedi thing because it's so powerful, then?"

Pimawa nudged the fish with his left foot, steering it wide around a clump of dead trees. "They were after the Eye of Dedi for many reasons. Power, however, was not one of them. Your parents believed that the Eye would restore magic to the Conjurian."

"I though you said this was a world for magicians. There's no magic here?" Alex demanded.

"Let him talk, Alex!" Emma scolded.

"Thank you," said Pimawa. "Magic is almost gone from our world. There are those who think the Eye might hold a way to return it. And there are those like"—he shuddered—"the Shadow Conjurer, who see the Eye as a chance to become the most powerful magician who remains."

"The Shadow Conjurer." Emma shivered too. "He's the one . . . with the scars on his face?"

"Exactly," Pimawa said.

"It seemed like he was kind of . . . after us?" she asked tentatively.

"You are correct, Miss Emma. He wished to capture you. In his mind, that would bring him closer to the Eye of Dedi."

"Why? Because he thinks that we know where it is or something? But we don't!" Emma protested.

"I know that. But the Shadow Conjurer does not," Pimawa answered.

"So I guess . . ." Emma's voice trailed off thoughtfully. "I guess we should try and find it, then. Before he gets it."

Both Alex and Pimawa stiffened in shock.

"You shall do no such thing!" Pimawa said sternly. "If your parents did indeed find the Eye—and we do not know that they did—they hid it to keep it out of the hands of magicians like the Shadow Conjurer. To keep it safe. They wanted to keep you safe as well, which is why they left you with Master Mordo. And my mission is to keep you that way by delivering you both to Master Agglar."

"That's where we're going? To Agglar?" Alex asked. "How's he supposed to keep us safe? He's just an antiques dealer like Uncle Mordo! Oh . . . except I guess you're about to tell me he isn't."

"Correct," answered Pimawa. "Christopher Agglar is the head of the Circle."

"Come on. Tell us what the Circle is," Alex said wearily.

"The Circle rules the Conjurian. It is a council of the most powerful magicians we have left," Pimawa answered.

Agglar and the others had been talking about the Circle, Alex remembered. Agglar had told Derren that if he left the house, he'd be thrown out of the Circle—and Derren had gone. Wait . . . so Derren Fallow was part of the Circle, too? Or he had been?

"Master Agglar will keep you both safe, Dedi permitting," Pimawa went on. He glanced over his shoulder nervously. "If only we can reach him."

"First of all, *safety* and *Master Agglar* should never be used in the same sentence," Alex told the rabbit, his words slipping out rapidly to hide how hard he was thinking. "He once told me he and Uncle Mordo needed privacy and to go play with the medieval ax collection in the basement." So Derren was part of this weird world too? And Derren didn't like Agglar. Didn't trust Agglar. "But yeah, Emma, Pimawa's totally right. This isn't one of your fantasy novels. We're not going off on a quest to find some Eye thing and save the world, okay?"

"Maybe *you're* not," Emma snapped.

"Listen to your brother," Pimawa told Emma. "And—"

His long ears twisted, as if he'd caught a sound. Then he kicked the fish hard, driving it to the right.

More fish burst from the mist behind them, an entire school swimming as fast as they could. In seconds they had overtaken the fish that Alex, Emma, and Pimawa were riding upon and had disappeared into the fog once more.

"They're in a hurry," said Alex, twisting around to try to see what might be behind them. "Usually a group of animals all running in one direction means—"

"Bandiloc!" yelled Pimawa as a furry head on a huge, snakelike body lashed out at them from the mist. Fangs raked at the fish's tail. The creature panicked and swerved hard to the left, flinging all three riders to the ground.

Pimawa scrambled to his feet, shoving the children behind him as the fish vanished into the mist. The furry gray head, like a rabid wolf's, drew back for another attack. "Run!" the rabbit shouted.

Alex wasn't sure if he could. The Myst fish had been weird, and the Rag-O-Rocs had been creepy, but this—this

was terrifying. Fear seemed to have grabbed hold of his entire body, and his legs didn't want to move.

He gripped Emma's arm, hypnotized by the monster's green eyes.

Pimawa leaped at the bandiloc's head. In midair he twisted, so that his powerful hind legs bashed the creature's nose. "RUN!" he bellowed.

Yes! Run! A great idea! Alex's legs sprang to life, but it was too late. A loop of the bandiloc's silvery snakelike body flung itself

over Alex and Emma, crushing them together. At the same time, the monster shook its head, sending Pimawa flying.

Then the head swung back to Emma and Alex. Its lower jaw opened wide and, with a strange, stomach-churning movement, dropped free from its hinge. Only stretchy skin now connected the lower jaw with the upper. The mouth sagged wider than should have been possible. Wide enough to swallow both Alex and Emma whole.

A flurry of white fur swept over Alex's head as Pimawa leaped onto the bandiloc's snout. The snarling head snapped backward, sending Pimawa soaring for a second time.

The snake's body cinched tighter around Alex's rib cage, and black spots burst in his vision. He couldn't draw in a full breath. He could, however, make out the fangs, inches from his face, dripping with wet clumps of venom. The smell of dead fish overwhelmed him.

Somewhere Alex had read that your life flashed in front of you before you died. But all Alex could see at the moment were the books in Uncle Mordo's library. Row upon row of them, holding what he used to think was all the knowledge in the world. But none of that knowledge was going to save him from being devoured by a wolf-headed snake.

Nor could Uncle Mordo's books tell him what the glowing blue eyes that had appeared out of the mist might belong to. It was something fast—that was all Alex could tell. And it was rushing closer and closer to them.

CHAPTER 4

EMMA

The air above Emma seemed to explode with orange fireworks at the same moment that something large collided with the bandiloc. The wolf-headed snake released the brother and sister, howling as it slid away into the mist.

Emma sat down hard on the rocky ground, sucking in as much air as she could. Alex landed beside her, but Emma could not spare much attention for her brother right then. She could not take her eyes off the contraption that had scared away their attacker.

It was made of metal and glass and wire. It was mechanical, and yet it almost seemed alive.

It was also an alpaca.

The alpaca pawed the moss with a metal hoof, gears

clicking and whirring inside its copper and steel frame. Then
its legs folded up, one after the other, and it collapsed slowly
to the ground as blue smoke spurted from its dented body.

The machine was tethered to a pear-shaped carriage,
much too large to be pulled by a flesh-and-blood animal. A
sign arching over the top of the carriage read GRUBIANS'
GRAND GUIGNOL. The alpaca chuffed more blue smoke and
cranked its head in all directions, as if watching for the bandiloc to return.

"What is that thing?" asked Emma. She could not help
smiling a little. The machine seemed so alive, she almost
wanted to reach out and pet it.

"Pure awesomeness!" Alex was grinning. Of course her

brother would love a machine like this, Emma thought. He was probably already figuring out how to build one of his own.

Emma watched as Alex got to his feet and came closer to the creature.

"Careful," Emma warned. "It might spit."

"Em, it's a machine," Alex scoffed. "They wouldn't build it to—"

A wad of bluish oil spattered on Alex's cheek. Emma couldn't help dissolving into peals of laughter. One day her brother might learn to listen to her!

Then a door in the carriage creaked open. Emma's laughter died. They had no idea who might be in there—or what. In every fantasy she'd ever read, a magical world had its perils.

"Alex! Watch out!" she called. It was so easy for her brother to get enthralled with some new mechanical contraption and forget anything else that might be going on. Like life-threatening danger.

Stairs covered in red carpet unfolded from the doorway. A huge, booted foot landed on the ground without touching any of the steps. The man attached to the foot straightened. Emma had to strain her neck back to look up at him. He was gigantic, eyes shadowed by the brim of his bowler hat.

"Whoa," said Alex. "Uh, hi?"

"We should go find Pimawa," whispered Emma.

"Pima who?" came a voice above them. A squat, barrel-shaped man hoisted himself out of a window to stand on the top of the carriage. "Well mighty, mighty mo, Clive! We have, I daresay, arrived in the nickiest nick of time." His smile seemed to extend beyond the sides of his rotund face.

The short man used Clive as a human ladder, landing with a dexterous spring on the ground.

"I am Neil Grubian," he said, smoothing back the greasy tuft of hair on his otherwise bald head. "This lamppost with ears is my brother, Clive."

Clive tipped his hat.

Neil shot his hand forward. "And who did we have the pleasure of saving from a crushing death this fine day?"

"Jane and Roger," said a firm voice from out of the mist. Pimawa limped into sight, his fur spiked with spots of dried

blood. He placed himself between the children and the Grubians. "We are indebted to you, truly. However, we must be moving on."

The short man sidled around Pimawa, squeezing himself between Alex and Emma. His stubby arms slipped over their shoulders.

"What I meant was," said Neil, "what are your *real* names?" He fixed Alex with a semiserious glare. "We've known each other for three minutes and already we're keeping secrets. My kind of people, Clive."

To Emma's surprise, Neil suddenly swung her away from Alex, holding on to her hand and spinning her like a ballerina. She wanted to pull away, but if she let go of his hand, she was afraid she'd fall, sprawling on the ground.

"They do not appear to be grateful, Clive," Neil remarked cheerfully. "Perhaps we should leave them for the bandiloc."

"Please, no," said Emma dizzily, trying to tug her hand out of Neil's. "We're grateful. Very grateful. It's just that—"

"What do you want?" demanded Pimawa.

Neil kissed Emma's hand and released her. He placed both hands over his chest. "Heartbreaking, Clive. Are we suspected of wanting something beyond gratitude for saving two lovely lives?"

Emma glanced guiltily at Alex. It was true—these men had saved them from that terrifying snakelike creature. What were they called? Bandilocs? It didn't seem fair to be suspicious in return, and yet . . .

Pimawa cleared his throat. He bowed. "Indeed. Our deepest thanks are owed to you both. And now—"

"Much appreciated," said Neil. "Still, what should we make of two youths wandering the Mysts in the company of a half-naked Jimjarian?"

"Please, we mean no disrespect," said Pimawa. He looked embarrassed as he tugged Emma's sweater tighter around his middle. "Obviously we could offer an outlandish tale, which I am certain you would dismiss immediately. Let us leave it at this. We have important business in Conjurian City and would be further indebted to you for transportation. However, for everyone's safety, we require anonymity."

Neil scaled the side of the carriage and seated himself on the top. His stubby legs dangled over the edge as he rested his ample head on his fist. "Myee, myee, my, Clive, we have stumbled upon a demanding group. Now, Clive and I do really enjoy a good secret. We especially love how valuable it can be." Neil opened his fist. Something bright and silver dangled from his fingers.

Alex's pocket watch! Emma gasped. She knew how much Alex loved that watch.

Her brother lunged forward, but Pimawa grabbed the collar of his shirt and snagged him back. "You will take us to Conjurian City," the rabbit said, holding Alex firmly. "And you will return the boy's watch. In return, we won't report you to the Circle."

The Circle, Emma remembered, ruled this strange and wonderful place. Christopher Agglar was in charge of it. But why was Pimawa threatening to turn these two men in to the Circle?

Neil cocked his head, then burst out laughing. "The almighty Circle! All hail Christopher Agglar and his merry band of blowhard clowns." Neil shook his head, then held his multiple chins high. "Why would you assume we fear the Circle?"

Pimawa kept a firm grip on Alex but craned his neck to peer into one of the rounded windows of the carriage. "Let us say Master Agglar has a keen interest in those who conduct business under cover of the Mysts."

"In that case, we'd best stay here, then," said Neil.

Emma didn't like the way they were looking at each other. And Alex was no help, glowering at everybody. It wasn't going to improve the situation to get into a big fight in the middle of this endless mist!

What if that horrible man with the scars on his face—the Shadow Conjurer—was following them? They needed to keep moving. And to keep moving, they'd need to do something about the metal alpaca now lying in a heap on the ground.

"Listen. None of us can go anywhere until we get this poor thing fixed," Emma said firmly. She reached out to stroke the alpaca's head.

"Ah, she does have a point," said Neil. "Right. Clive, put my tea on for me. Looks like we're having a holiday."

"It's not a poor thing, Em. It's a broken machine. And I can fix it," said Alex. He shook Pimawa's hand off his collar.

"Her name is Gertie," said Neil.

"I can help fix Gertie in exchange for a ride," said Alex. "*And* my watch back. That's a deal? You get your machine repaired, and I get my watch back, and nobody gets reported to the Circle." He glanced up at Pimawa. "Everybody wins."

Neil slid off the carriage. His brother caught him and placed him down in front of Pimawa. The shorter brother circled around the giant rabbit and handed the watch over to Alex.

Alex had just better be as good with machines as he always bragged he was, Emma thought. Or none of them would be going anywhere.

ALEX

"She runs on *magic*?" Alex asked, prying a bandiloc tooth out of a gear that made one of Gertie's knees bend.

"What else would power a mechanized alpaca?" Neil passed Alex an enormous wrench.

"Oh, I don't know," said Alex. He whacked the wrench against a bolt. "Gasoline, propane, electricity, solar, steam. Things that actually exist."

"How did such a young skeptic end up in the Conjurian?" asked Neil.

One look from Pimawa reminded Alex to keep his mouth closed.

Neil mimed zipping his lips shut. "Oh, right. That's top-secret, apparently."

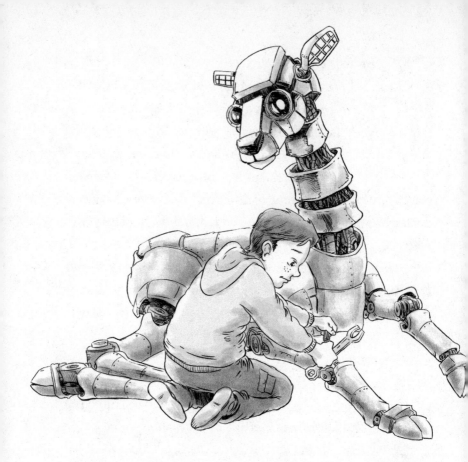

Alex gave the bolt one more whack, then threaded an iron gear on top. He tightened the nut, locking the gear in place. Gertie rose up on all four legs, flexing her repaired joint. She hopped in place twice, then nuzzled the top of Alex's head.

"Okay, okay, you're welcome," said Alex, patting Gertie's cheek.

"Just a machine, huh?" Emma asked, poking her head out one of the carriage's windows. She smirked at Alex.

"The second joint in her neck will need new bearings, but her leg should go for a long time," Alex told Neil, ignoring his sister. "Where do we fuel her up?"

With a gleaming smile, Neil unlatched Gertie's rib cage and lifted it open, exposing a glowing blue canister.

"Whoa." Alex leaned in, face awash in the faint blue light. "What is that? Is that plasma?" He jerked his head back. "Is it radioactive?"

Emma jumped down from the carriage to look too.

"It's magic," said Neil. "But she's a touch low. If we let her charge up for half an hour or so, it should be enough to get us to the city."

"Magic," Emma breathed, wide-eyed. "Wow."

Alex gave her an impatient look. "By magic, you mean you don't know how it works," he said to Neil.

"Oh, I know how it works," said Neil, swatting Alex's greasy hand away from the canister. "See, we all have a bit of magic in us. Some of us more than others, but none very much, not these days. Soon enough, it will all be gone."

"Where did you get that?" Pimawa jabbed a finger at the glowing canister. "The Circle has banned such devices!"

Neil closed Gertie's chest. "You needn't ruffle your cotton tail. Devices such as this one will soon be obsolete. No fuel, no go. Aces alive, it takes us several months to collect half a tank."

Alex reached for the latch as Emma backed away. "Let me see it." Whatever that blue stuff really was, he wanted to figure out how it gave Gertie her power.

Pimawa grabbed his wrist.

"Let go!" Alex twisted his arm. "Hey! I need to see how it works!" How was he supposed to keep Gertie running if he didn't understand her power source?

"What we need," said Pimawa, "is to be on our way to the Tower." He lowered his voice. "Please, Master Alex. Remember who may be on our tail."

Alex was quite prepared to argue some more, no matter how many villains with blue faces might be chasing them— but just then something orange exploded in the air over his head with a bang that hurt his eardrums. Gasping in alarm, Pimawa shoved him to the ground and fell on top of him.

Alex lay half under Pimawa, looking around for the new threat. What had made that noise? A gun? A bomb? And where was Emma?

"Whoops," Emma said. "Sorry." She was standing a few paces away, shamefaced, with a purple silk pouch in her hand.

"What *was* that?" Alex squirmed out from under Pimawa and sat up. His heart was still thumping.

Emma held up what looked like a pumpkin seed.

Pimawa sighed. "Really, Miss Emma. You do not quite understand—"

"Put that down!" Neil interrupted. "Clive, did you give those to her? You have the sense of a featherless parrot!"

With a guilty frown, Clive confiscated the pouch from Emma.

"You used these to scare the bandiloc," said Alex, remembering. He'd seen that same orange flash right before Gertie had crashed into the wolf-snake monster.

"They're called woofle seeds," said Neil. "Clive, give them here before you lose a finger." He snatched the pouch from his brother and tucked it into his vest. "Those aren't to be trifled with, young Jane." He wagged a finger at Emma. "They grow high in the mountains. Hard to come by. Back in the day, all the magicians used them. Quite common. These days, certain non-magic clients pay hefty fees for them."

"Sorry," said Emma. "I found them in the carriage. It wasn't Clive's fault. I just wondered what they'd do. If they were . . . you know, magic. Like Gertie. I've never seen real magic before."

"Oh my, pie in the sky," said Neil. "'Tis a show you want? We have a spot of time to kill while Gertie catches her breath. We can accommodate. No extra charge! Places, Clive! Hup to it!" The short man ushered them around to a large wooden cabinet protruding from the back of the carriage. The top half unfolded into a small stage with faded red curtains, flanked by two iron lanterns.

"Welcome to our humble theater!" Neil announced,

flinging his arms wide. "The greatest show on . . . well, *in* the Mysts."

Neil opened a door on the side of the carriage, and he and his brother slipped inside. Alex exchanged a glance with Emma, then shrugged and sat on the ground beside her. Pimawa fidgeted behind them, his ears swiveling as he listened for sounds in the mists.

Alex knew the rabbit was nervous and wanted them to be moving along—but if Neil was right, they couldn't move along, not until Gertie was charged up. They might as well watch, he figured. Not much else to do.

It seemed that there was not much to watch, either. Nothing happened for several seconds. Then the faded red curtains parted. Neil's voice, slightly muffled, came from inside the cabinet as a plain wooden puppet, thin and knobby-limbed, danced onto the stage. "Dedi was the most powerful magician in all of Egypt. One day he performed his greatest feat for the Pharaoh. He removed the head of a goose and then brought it back to life!"

Alex squinted. He knew there must be strings attached to the puppet, but he saw none. Probably because of all the shadows created by the flickering lanterns.

A beautiful puppet with long black hair sashayed onto the stage as Neil's narration continued. "Shortly after, the queen fell ill and died." The puppet fell to the stage as if her strings had been cut, except that Alex could still see no strings.

"Pharaoh was devastated. He commanded Dedi to bring her back to life!" Neil announced. A tall puppet in a golden headdress confronted the frail form of the magician. The magician puppet shook its wooden head. "Dedi tried to explain that restoring the goose was merely a trick. He told the Pharaoh that using real magic to revive the dead would lead down a dark and dangerous path.

"The Pharaoh clapped Dedi into a prison cell," declared Neil. The puppet in the golden headdress swept off the stage, and the smaller puppet huddled sadly on the floor. "Each day that Dedi refused to bring the queen back from the land of the dead, a member of Dedi's family was thrown into a pit of vipers!"

A trapdoor in the middle of the stage slid open. Another female puppet and several smaller ones appeared, only to

promptly vanish down the trapdoor. Harrowing cries came from backstage. Emma winced. Alex rolled his eyes.

"Each night, in his cell, Dedi began transferring all his power into a single pebble. Several more days passed, until, finally, Dedi was ready."

A very small puppet ventured hesitantly onto the stage and wavered on the edge of the trapdoor.

"Right before his youngest daughter was about to tumble into the pit, Dedi cast the stone down!" Neil cried dramatically. A plume of bluish smoke wafted up through the trapdoor, and when it had drifted away, every puppet was gone from the stage. "He vanished with his remaining family in a stream of blue light. Using the magic in that stone, Dedi had created a world far away. A world of magic. A sanctuary for Dedi and his

family. With the stone, Dedi had created the Conjurian."

A canvas screen painted with an image of a tree unrolled along the back of the stage as Neil's voice wound up his narration.

"Dedi sacrificed all his power to build our world, and put whatever might remain of his magic in what we now call the Eye of Dedi so that other sorcerers could escape perse-cution. He planted a tree on the spot where he first set foot in the Conjurian. A living, growing reminder of why this world was created, and what our livelihood was worth."

The curtains swept back over the stage. Clive rose from the top of the cabinet, holding his hat as he bowed. A panel below the stage slid open to reveal Neil, crammed into a compartment crowded with gears and pulleys. Alex would have liked to take a closer look at all the mechanisms, but Neil sprang out and shut the panel smartly behind him. Then he took a bow.

Emma jumped to her feet, clapping furiously. *Of course she did*, Alex thought. *It was just the kind of story she liked—exciting, tragic, and completely implausible.*

He clapped too, though, for a different reason. Pimawa smiled and offered some polite applause as well.

"Thank you, thank you! Much too kind," said Neil, taking several more bows. He winked at Alex. "Young man, what did you think?"

"It was amazing," said Alex. He meant it. "How did you hide the strings? How did you make that blue smoke? Can I go under the stage?"

"You are made of questions, my boy," said Neil, tapping Alex on the forehead. "However, we still owe you a ride to town. Gertie's ready, and we'd best be off before it gets too late. Everyone aboard!"

CHAPTER 5

EMMA

Emma sniffed as she settled down in a corner of the carriage, with Pimawa beside her. The place smelled of cranberries and old newspapers. It was crammed with television boxes, toaster ovens, microwaves, and laptops.

It was also rocking very gently as Gertie pranced ahead, pulling them through the mists. Neither Clive nor Neil seemed to be driving—maybe Gertie just knew her own way.

Clive and Alex sat on the cushioned seat across from Emma and Pimawa.

"Clive! Put some tea on," barked Neil from somewhere behind Emma. "Horrible host, that one."

"What do they need all this stuff for?" Emma whispered to Pimawa as Clive pulled a teapot from under his seat, got to his feet, and removed several teacups from inside a top hat.

"They don't," said Pimawa. "They smuggle it in from the Flatworld. Do *not* touch anything."

"Flatworld?" asked Emma.

"Yes!" Neil popped up suddenly close behind them, making Emma gasp and jump. "The Flatworld. The world that persecuted magicians for eons and now no longer believes in magic. Flatworlders do so love our exotic goods, though." Neil gestured at the stacked boxes. "Three woofle seeds and a dancing cane got us all of this."

"You don't have TVs in the Conjurian?" asked Emma.

"We do now." Neil slapped one of the boxes.

"Why do you have to sneak them in?" Emma reached for a jar full of bright green goo.

Pimawa swatted her hand. "Don't touch that!"

Neil sighed heavily. "Our dear Master Agglar banned it all."

"Agglar? You mean, like, Christopher Agglar?" Alex asked. He turned toward them, holding a small cage. Something invisible inside squeaked, battering wildly against the thin bars.

"For Dedi's sake, stop touching stuff!" Pimawa snatched the cage and thrust it toward Neil.

"Of course. It is Master Agglar who heads the Circle, and the Circle, of course, rules us all." Neil eyed Alex with a

calculating curiosity. "It's odd that you do not know something that every child in the Conjurian knows."

"Why would he ban toaster ovens?" asked Emma.

"That is something you should ask Master Agglar. Will you be paying a call on him when you reach Conjurian City?" asked Neil, his eyes bright and inquisitive.

"Excellent idea," said Pimawa, without answering. "Let us save *all* questions until we get to Conjurian City."

A silence stretched out, making Emma's toes twitch. Surely Pimawa didn't expect that nobody would say a word until they got wherever they were going. She squirmed in her seat and spotted something tacked up to the wall of the carriage. "A map!" she said with a little more excitement than she meant to show. Pimawa wouldn't mind her looking at a map. Right?

Alex also seemed intrigued. He came over to peer at the piece of parchment with Emma. "Looks like the coast of Maine," he said. "How come so much of it is unlabeled?"

"Ah, I didn't think you'd be able to resist more questions," said Neil with a smirk. He handed Emma a cup of tea. "Much of it is unexplored."

"But you said in that puppet show that this world was

created thousands of years ago," Alex said. "No one's gone poking around?"

"Oh, they have," said Neil. "A lot of them don't come back."

Pimawa's ears twitched, and he bent closer to the map. Emma had to edge back out of the way. "These markings," he said. "Are they all forbidden gateways?"

"Like the one you snuck through?" Neil stuck another pin in the map.

"Great, we're trespassers," muttered Alex.

"Far from it," said Pimawa. He eyed Neil sternly. "*We* entered the Conjurian out of dire necessity." Pimawa pointed to a spot that marked the Tower of Dedi. "Here. This is the only official entrance into our world."

"Unless you are one of the privileged few who have their own personal gateway," said Neil. "Takes a lot of magic to make one. More than most people have nowadays. How did you come by yours?"

"Children." Pimawa shooed both Emma and Alex away

from the map. "I suggest you rest on the journey to the city. Is there somewhere they could—"

Behind Pimawa, Clive had placed three beanbag chairs, price tags still attached.

Emma would have liked to study the map longer. She would have liked to learn more about this world, about the Circle, about the Shadow Conjurer and the Eye he was supposed to be searching for. Most of all, she'd have liked to ask Pimawa why he seemed to be so determined to mistrust Neil and Clive. The Grubians had saved them from the snake creature, the bandiloc, hadn't they? And they seemed nice enough.

But it was clear that Pimawa didn't want them to talk to the two brothers. And Uncle Mordo had told them to follow

Pimawa. Emma handed Clive her empty teacup and slumped onto a beanbag with a sigh. Alex, after failing to contain a yawn, dropped into the chair next to Emma's.

But when Clive attempted to guide Pimawa to the last beanbag, Pimawa didn't budge.

"No thank you. I shall remain standing." Pimawa flashed a stern look at the tall man. "And awake."

"Well, then," said Neil, pressing a bundle of folded cloth to Pimawa's chest. "At least have the decency to put some clothes on."

Begrudgingly, Pimawa thanked them. He sniffed the pile of clothing cautiously.

"Don't thank me," Neil said with a smile that was too wide to be friendly. "You have no idea where I got them."

Shouts and bells woke Emma from her slumber. Fighting pins and needles, she struggled out of the beanbag chair and stuck her head out one of the carriage's round windows, squinting against the rays of morning sun.

The carriage had stopped, since the road was jammed with every kind of vehicle Emma could imagine. Some of them she was pretty sure she *couldn't* have imagined. Steam-powered bicycles idled next to antique cars that had mechanical legs instead of wheels. Carts pulled by metal ostriches or giraffes jockeyed for positions with rickshaws dragged by unicyclists. The sidewalk overflowed with a stream of people wearing top hats, turbans, quilted robes, ball gowns, and ponchos. Emma even spotted a few men in tuxedos.

She couldn't help grinning. She'd read more books than she could count, all of them full of scenes like this. And even if some horrible guy called the Shadow Conjurer was after her and her brother, even if her uncle was . . . Emma didn't finish the thought. She didn't really want to think about what her uncle was.

Even if all that was true, what she was seeing was still amazing.

"Alex, get up." She nudged her brother with a toe. "You're going to want to see this!"

After several mumbled protests and a foot in the ribs, Alex joined her at the window.

"A bakery!" Emma pointed at a shop window with shelves of brightly colored pastries. "Let's go check it out while we're stopped."

"Absolutely not! Get away from the window right now!" Pimawa, who had been crouched on his own beanbag, bounced up and put a paw on Emma's shoulder and one on Alex's. But he didn't pull them away from the window. Instead he stood looking, just as they were. Slowly, his ears drooped until they were dangling down his back.

"How long have you been away?" asked Emma, a little shyly. It was funny to think of Pimawa—her pet rabbit—having had a life here, in this city, long before she'd known him.

"Too long," said Pimawa, still staring.

"Must be good to be home again," Emma suggested.

"It would be, if it were the same home I'd left."

What on earth did Pimawa mean by that? Emma longed

to ask, but before she could, an eager voice rang out. "Master Fornesworth!" someone called from outside the window. Emma saw three young rabbits—Jimjarians, she assumed—scuttling toward the carriage.

"Master Fornesworth, sir," the first one repeated. He lifted his bowler hat politely. "Is that you?"

"Pimawa Fornesworth, assistant to Mordo the Mystifier!" said the second. He poked the third in the ribs. "Told you it was him!"

"You said he was dead," the third quipped.

"I did not!" said the second. "I said he was still in the Flatworld."

"Sir, it is an honor to meet you!" the first of the Jimjarians offered, bowing slightly. "I am Rofflo Penwedge, and these two, well—ignore them."

"Is Master Mordo inside?" asked the third.

"Don't be rude," said Rofflo as he pulled himself to the window. "Between me and you, Master Fornesworth, these two don't stand a chance at the Choosing ceremony."

"Away," said Pimawa. "The three of you!" He swatted at Rofflo's furry paws.

Rofflo dodged Pimawa and stuck his face through the window a second time. "Sir," he asked, "is it true? The Shadow Conjurer took out two members of the Circle? It's in all the papers." His whiskers quivered nervously. "Will he come . . . here next? To Conjurian City? Master Agglar will protect us, I'm sure. Of course. But—"

Pimawa slammed the window shut, very nearly slicing off Rofflo's fingers in the process. "No magician in their right mind would ever select the likes of those three ruffians," he muttered.

"What's the Choosing?" asked Alex. He tried sidestepping Pimawa for another peek out the window.

"It is the most important moment in a Jimjarian's life." Pimawa blocked him. "I trained hard for my ceremony. I was tremendously proud to be chosen by your uncle. I certainly wasn't running amok through the city harassing respectable citizens."

"Well, well, well." Emma turned away from the window at the sound of Neil's voice. Alex and Pimawa looked around too. The smaller Grubian smiled up at them from one of the beanbags. "I had no idea we were transporting such an esteemed passenger. Pimawa Fornesworth. Jimjarian to Mordo the Mystifier. Do tell. *Did* that mysterious Shadow Conjurer wipe out our precious Circle? Or is that just the tale you've been instructed to spread?"

Emma was beginning to feel that she did not like Neil at all—even if he *had* saved her from being eaten by a bandiloc. "It's not a tale," she said firmly. "We saw the Shadow Conjurer. Pimawa saved us from him."

"How delightfully fortuitous," Neil said thoughtfully. "The Shadow Conjurer strikes, and everyone runs to Master Agglar for protection."

"I do not appreciate your insinuations," said Pimawa. "We'll thank you to finish your end of our deal, and that will be the last we need to see of each other."

"I wish for nothing else myself," said Neil. "However, the city is in a bit of a hubbub this morning." He whipped a rolled-up newspaper from his back pocket and snapped it open with a flourish. Emma leaned forward to read over his shoulder. Pimawa did the same.

"It's not looking good, people. The streets are clogged worse than a constipated elephant. Not to mention all the Tower guards roaming about like cockroaches," said Neil. "It seems that people are a trifle . . . unsettled. They do get ever so jumpy when they hear any mention of the Shadow Conjurer. My, but they do. And we have not quite . . . tidied up our carriage for an inspection. So we cannot bring you to the Tower. However, we shall take you someplace much safer."

Emma didn't exactly like the sound of that. Much safer for herself and Alex and Pimawa? Or for Neil and Clive?

"You are aware of the danger facing these children!" said Pimawa, pointing at the newspaper. "You must deliver them safely to Master Agglar. He is the only one who can protect them!"

"No can do." Neil rolled up the newspaper again and swatted at a fly buzzing over his head.

"Then, good sir, we thank you for your services and shall take our leave right here." Pimawa straightened his newly acquired jacket. "Master Alex, Miss Emma. Come."

Pimawa didn't seem to notice the smile that spread across Neil's face as he said those two names. But Emma did. She stayed close to Pimawa

as he flung the carriage door open. He hopped onto the packed street.

Halfway down the steps, Emma felt a twinge of doubt. Neil and Clive *had* saved her and Alex, after all. And gotten them to the city as well. She paused to look back and smile. "Thank you."

Her smile faded as she saw Alex standing at the top of the stairs, next to Neil, with a look on his face that she recognized all too well.

"Wait," Alex called to Pimawa. "We shouldn't go to the Tower."

"Wisdom from the mouth of a babe!" Neil laid his arm across Alex's shoulders. "I assure you, we can bring you somewhere safe. Somewhere Agglar can't get his arthritic hands on you."

"Come out this instant!" Pimawa ordered Alex.

"No. I don't trust Agglar," said Alex. His jaw was set stubbornly. Emma hesitated on the steps. Should she join Pimawa on the streets? Go back up and argue with Alex? But it was no use arguing with him when his face looked like that. She knew that all too well.

"You trust *him*?" Pimawa jabbed a finger toward Neil.

"I don't know who to trust. Not yet," said Alex. "Derren will know. We need to find him."

Pimawa shook his head in exasperation. "You should trust your uncle," the rabbit said. "He gave you into my care and told me to take you to the Tower."

"Yeah, we tried trusting Uncle Mordo," said Alex. "Look where that got us."

"Alex!" Emma, still halfway down the stairs, couldn't stay quiet. "Uncle Mordo died to save us!"

Alex looked embarrassed. "Okay, I know, Em, but still—"

"He's right over there!" called out a high, shrill voice. The three young Jimjarians who'd come to the carriage window earlier were talking to a cluster of guards in gray uniforms. They pointed at Pimawa.

"Alex, come on!" Emma hissed. She jumped down the remaining stairs to Pimawa's side just as the guards reached them. A stocky man, the only one of the group with a red band on his hat, stepped forward, smacking a baton against his palm. "Alex and Emma Maskelyne, you are coming with us."

Neil's eyes flashed and his arm tightened around Alex. "Quickly, back inside."

But Clive, leaning out the window, caught his brother's eye and nodded toward Gertie. Two guards had stepped up to her, and one had pried open her chest plate. Blue sparks shot out as he yanked wires loose from the glowing blue tube that powered her engine.

It was clear to Emma that the carriage wasn't going anywhere. She looked anxiously up at Pimawa. Who were these men? Should they go with them? Did they have a choice?

"Good morning, sir." Pimawa bowed to the guard with the red-banded hat. "I'm Master Pimawa Fornesworth, assistant to Mordo the Mystifier. And to whom do I have the pleasure of—"

"I'm Sergeant Miller," the man interrupted him. "And

you and the children are now under the protection of the Circle." He snapped his fingers. Two of his men grabbed Pimawa, lifting him off the ground. At the same time, Emma felt powerful hands take hold of her arms and hoist her into the air.

"Hey!" Emma shouted. "That hurts! Stop!" She kicked, but her feet touched nothing.

"Don't touch her!" Alex yelled. He twisted out from under Neil's arm and leaped from the carriage. Emma would have been more touched and pleased by this if another guard had not grabbed Alex before he hit the ground. The man held her brother pinned with an arm around his chest. "Bug off!" Alex snapped. He squirmed and twisted uselessly.

"Nothing to see here, people." The sergeant waved his baton at the onlookers.

"Pardon me!" Neil sauntered down the carriage steps, clutching a small silk pouch. Emma recognized it and stopped struggling.

Casually Neil raised the little bag of woofle seeds high in the air.

Emma braced herself for the explosion as a voice shouted from above her head:

"Stop! Thief!"

A boy tumbled from a third-story window. He managed to snag a drain-pipe, slowing his descent. Then he bounced off a striped awning and landed on Sergeant Miller.

The two fell, sprawling on the ground, but since he was on top, the boy was the first to move. Springing off the prone officer, he seized Emma, keeping her between him and the rest of the enraged guards.

"Morning," said the boy. "I'm Savachia. Hate to impose, but I'm rather in need of a hostage."

STOP! THIEF!

CHAPTER 6

ALEX

Alex and Pimawa trudged through the crowd, which parted to let them pass. No one seemed to want to argue with the platoon of guards that surrounded them.

"Do not fret, Master Alex," Pimawa said under his breath. "The escort is merely a security precaution."

Alex had some serious doubts about that. The fact that he and Pimawa were chained together was a hint that the guards were not just looking out for their welfare.

"All this will be straightened out once we are before Master Agglar," Pimawa continued. "I guarantee Sergeant Miller has already sent men to rescue Miss Emma."

Sergeant Miller prodded both of them with his baton. "Keep quiet and walk faster."

Alex wanted to say something rude, but he feared his voice would tremble if he thought too much about what had happened to his sister. He might even start to cry.

Emma drove him crazy sometimes, no doubt about that. Her stubborn belief that their parents were coming back any day now made Alex want to grab her and shake her and force her to face facts.

But she was all the family he had. His parents were gone, even if Emma wouldn't admit it. Now his uncle was too. Alex had never been fond of Uncle Mordo—how could anybody be fond of Uncle Mordo?—but he'd been there. He'd been stern, dictatorial, impatient, and as reliable as the earth beneath Alex's feet. However Alex might have felt about his uncle's rules and lectures, Mordo had always been around.

Until now.

Emma was all Alex had left. But that boy had grabbed her, and they'd both vanished. Like magic, Emma would have said.

A day ago, Alex would have scoffed at her, would have pointed out all the ways the trick might have been managed with props and clever camera angles and sleight of hand. But now he had to admit it—in this crazy place, magic might actually be real. And it might have taken his sister away from him.

That didn't mean he had to like it.

Alex treaded along in silence behind Pimawa as they crossed a rusted iron bridge over the murky sea. Abandoned warehouses lined one bank of the water, Alex noticed. They went on into the heart of the city. The air grew salty and smelled a bit like oil. Most of the storefronts they passed were boarded up. The wind whistled through their broken windows.

BENJAMIN RUCKER'S
ASRAH FACTORY

Alex could see what he figured must be their destination, the Tower of Dedi, rising over rooftops and chimneys. Its upper tiers were hidden by a mix of clouds and smog. The closer they got, the fewer people they encountered. And those who were milling about were quick to retreat into the shadows at the sight of the Tower guards.

Alex, Pimawa, and their captors passed the last of the buildings and reached a grassy field. Things that looked like petrified sea serpents arched from the ground. As they got closer, Alex saw that they were in fact the roots of a colossal tree. The trunk, wider around than a city block, formed the base of the Tower.

Once Alex's guards had escorted him among the roots, up a flight of stone stairs, and through a pair of giant doors, he found himself inside the heart of the giant tree. It was hollow. He stood in a cylindrical chamber with wooden walls and a floor worn smooth over the centuries. A slender box, taller than Alex, stood in the center with men in gray uniforms on either side.

As Alex and Pimawa were herded toward a winding staircase on the far side of the chamber, the box fizzled with blue light. The light faded, and a guard opened the door, yanking out an old man in a moth-chewed tuxedo.

"A new arrival," whispered Pimawa, stopping. "Let's see how he does."

"Does what?" asked Alex.

Their guards seemed curious too. They allowed their prisoners to stop to watch the proceedings.

"Perform," answered Pimawa. "Anyone trying to enter the Conjurian must prove they have true magical abilities, not just some sleight of hand they learned in a book."

Alex eyed Pimawa skeptically. "You mean he's going to levitate or something?"

"Gracious, no," said Pimawa. "No one's had power like that in ages. The simplest effect will do. So long as he uses

real magic." He sighed. "I doubt many people get in these days."

Intrigued, Alex watched as the old man whisked a yellowed handkerchief from his breast pocket. He flourished the handkerchief as best he could. His fingers seemed stiff, the knuckles swollen.

"Get on with it," snapped one of the guards.

The old man's lips quivered as he tucked the handkerchief into his fist. One finger at a time, his hand opened. The handkerchief was gone. He managed a proud smile.

"Seriously?" The guard reached over and pulled the man's jacket open, revealing the handkerchief tucked into a small pouch dangling from an elastic strap around his arm. "Right, bring him below."

"Wait!" the old man gasped. "I swear, I used to have magic, but it's gone. It went away. My name is Harold the Great. Please, someone here must have heard of me!"

The guard seized hold of the man by the collar of his black jacket, ignoring his pleas, and walked him away from the box and through a door in the wooden wall. On the door, Alex could make out the words CON-JURIAN DETENTION CENTER. Something smaller that Alex couldn't read was printed underneath.

The door shut behind Harold the Great, cutting off his anxious voice.

Alex nearly shivered. Okay, the old man had

been a fraud, obviously—but it was just a stupid magic trick. Or non-magic trick. Not a huge crime or anything. But the guards had seemed so grim. . . .

"What's going to happen to him?" he asked nervously.

"Never you mind," Sergeant Miller snapped. He shoved Alex toward the winding staircase. "Keep moving."

Alex marched behind Pimawa up the curving staircase, which began to seem endless. After each full turn, they'd pass a landing with a doorway that led into a hall branching out from the center of the Tower. Alex kept hoping they'd reached the right door and would be getting off the staircase, but each time, the guards herded him and Pimawa farther up.

The walls changed from wood to stone to stucco and, eventually, modern drywall. Alex glanced out every window they passed at the sprawling city. After a time, all he could see were drizzly clouds.

His legs ached, then trembled, then started to feel as if they had been filled with syrup. Yet anytime he tried to pause for a breath, the guards jerked him up more stairs.

"Why don't you have elevators?" he groaned.

"Why don't you have your Jimjarian carry you?" A guard behind him snickered.

Just when Alex felt as if his knees would buckle, Sergeant Miller finally allowed them all to rest. Alex flopped down to sit on the stairs, and his captors let him do it, although he had a feeling it wouldn't be long enough to really catch his breath.

They were on a landing with an open doorway that led into a hall jammed with boxes and dusty cabinets. Along the corridor, Alex saw a metal door secured with a rusted padlock. The letters on the door made him forget all about his burning lungs.

Alex had heard about those letters before. Pimawa had mentioned them. *MAGE* stood for *Magic Antiquities Guardianship and Enforcement*. The rabbit had claimed that Alex and Emma's parents had not been archaeologists after all—that they'd been some kind of magical secret agents. And behind that door was the place where they had worked!

"Get moving," Sergeant Miller grunted, tugging on the chains around Alex's hands and pulling him upright. "Master Agglar's waiting for you."

Alex did not want to move away from that door. There might be clues of all kinds behind it—clues to what his parents had really been doing and what had happened to them. Nobody asked him what he wanted, however, and all he could do was count the landings they passed, making sure to remember how many floors separated him from the MAGE office and all that it contained.

"Almost there," said Pimawa, trying to sound reassuring, as if they were taking a relaxing stroll through Uncle Mordo's gardens.

Seven floors, and one hundred and sixty-eight steps later, they came to a stop. The stairs did not go any farther, Alex could see. They had to be at the very top of the Tower.

This landing did not have an open doorway leading to a hall, like all the others. Instead he saw a pair of white doors with golden doorknobs, firmly closed.

Sergeant Miller opened them and pulled on the chains, leading Alex and Pimawa into the room beyond.

Alex took in everything he could see. The room was circular. The walls were filled with framed posters of magicians. A round table with a shining marble surface took up most of the space. Thirteen empty chairs were drawn up to it.

Eight windows stretched from the floor to the domed ceiling. Near one of them, Christopher Agglar leaned on his cane. A few feet away stood a tall, burly Jimjarian.

Sergeant Miller gave Agglar a brief military bow. He dropped the end of the chain connected to Alex's shackles and turned to go.

The last guard in line chuckled as he filed out behind the others. "Last stop. Feel free to pass out now," he muttered to Alex.

Then he closed the door behind him, leaving Alex and

Pimawa alone in the room with Agglar and the unknown Jimjarian.

"Please, come closer," said Agglar. He nodded to his Jimjarian. "Rowlfin, if you would."

Rowlfin approached, his furry chin held high as he withdrew a key from his waistcoat. He unlocked Alex's shackles first. Then, with a stern glare, he freed Pimawa.

"Greetings, Father," said Pimawa, rubbing his furry wrists.

Rowlfin let out a disapproving sound, sort of like "Chuff!" He slung the chains over his shoulder and returned to Agglar's side.

Alex turned his head to look at Pimawa in surprise. This other giant rabbit was Pimawa's father? What kind of a greeting was that between father and son?

Pimawa looked at the floor. He seemed to be trying to avoid Alex's gaze.

"Please," said Agglar, turning from the window, "have a look around."

There were two things Alex did not want to do at that moment. The first one was to take another step. And the second was to do anything that Christopher Agglar told him to.

But he needed a moment, and not just to catch his breath. He needed to sort his thoughts out. Seeing his uncle's old antiques-dealer crony standing here, in this crazy tower made out of a tree, acting like he owned the place—maybe he *did* own the place?—made Alex's brain spin a little.

He needed to understand what was happening here. He needed answers. And old Agglar was going to give them to him.

He'd just take a moment to figure out the right questions.

Alex stuffed both hands into his pockets. In the right one, he felt his father's old watch, and he rubbed his fingers over its smooth surface as he limped forward on his aching legs. He looked at the portraits on the walls without really seeing them as he tried to figure out what to ask first.

But one portrait riveted his attention, and his questions fell out of his mind. In it, a woman with chestnut-brown hair to her shoulders was sitting on an armchair, leaning a little to one side. A tall man stood behind her, one arm on the chair's back. She had her head tilted up a little, so that she could meet his eyes. His face was turned slightly down to hers.

Alex gripped the watch tightly. He was looking at his parents.

"An ever-growing gallery of those who made the ultimate sacrifice for magic," said Agglar, watching Alex closely. "Sadly, we will be adding a portrait of your uncle next to the one of your parents. Sit." He gestured toward the chairs with his cane.

Pimawa sat obediently. Alex didn't move.

Agglar crossed the room, leaning on his cane with each step, until he stood uncomfortably close to Alex. "Open your hand," he said shortly.

Alex didn't budge.

With a hiss of impatience, Agglar seized the boy's wrist and turned his hand over so that his open palm was on top. Then he placed a silver coin on Alex's palm. Opening his own hand, he displayed a copper coin. "Transpose them," he said shortly.

"You want me to switch the coins?" Alex reached for the copper coin with his free hand.

Agglar slapped his hand away. "Using magic."

Alex was speechless. This old man was crazier than he had ever imagined. Okay, Alex might have to admit that there was something in this world, some kind of force, that he didn't understand—something that powered Gertie, that made seeds explode and fish swim through mist and trees grow as big as the Empire State Building. Fine. He'd call that force *magic* if he had to.

But what on earth made Christopher Agglar think Alex could do a thing with that force? With . . . magic?

He shrugged and he handed the silver coin back. "I have no idea what you mean."

Agglar's eyes narrowed. "I had hoped that, despite your sheltered upbringing, you would show some natural ability for conjuring," he said. "Regardless, if you *do* hold any clues to the Eye of Dedi's location, I will extract them."

Alex narrowed his own eyes. "That Eye thing? I don't have any idea where it is. Or what it is. Listen, I want to know—"

He wanted to know so many things.

Like, where was Emma? What was Agglar doing to get her back?

And who was that Shadow Conjurer guy? Why did he think that Alex and Emma might know anything about the Eye?

And why did Agglar think the same thing? That Alex might have some kind of clue about the Eye?

And if Agglar was really a friend of Uncle Mordo's—if Agglar was supposed to keep both Alex and Emma safe—then why had Alex been brought here in chains?

But before Alex could ask anything, Pimawa stepped forward. "Master Agglar, might I suggest a bit of rest for the young Maskelyne? It has been a trying morning."

Both Rowlfin and Agglar glared at Pimawa.

"You dare tell me what needs to be done! This is how you respect the memory of your master?" Agglar demanded.

"Sir, no," said Pimawa. "I only—"

"Hold your tongue!" Rowlfin snapped.

Pimawa's ears drooped flat behind his head.

"Hey," Alex said angrily. "What are you—"

Agglar stepped toward Alex and bent over, his long nose inches from Alex's face. Alex stopped talking.

Agglar studied Alex and then nodded. "So he's tired? Very well. Rowlfin, lock him up in suitable quarters for napping. We shall have his sister shortly."

CHAPTER 7

EMMA

Emma dragged herself out of a manhole onto a crowded cobblestone street. People hardly seemed to notice her, or to care that she'd arrived in such an unusual way. They just streamed around her, nudging and pushing, grumbling for her to get out of the way.

She knew she ought to run. She had to escape. But every time she took a step, someone bumped or jostled her back toward the hole she'd climbed out of.

Once the boy had grabbed Emma, a white haze had exploded all around them. When it had cleared, they'd been together in an old stone tunnel. She'd wrenched free and started running, then spotted the ladder. It had only taken her a few moments to climb up and shove the manhole cover aside.

She knew the boy was close behind her. At any minute he would grab her. She had to run . . . but which way?

All around her, buildings leaned like rotted stumps, blocking any view of the only landmark she knew, the Tower of Dedi. But she could see a side street nearby. She darted toward it, only to slam into a hunchbacked man wearing a top hat held together by safety pins. He shoved her back the way she'd come.

"Watch where you're going," he snarled.

"Good to see you're making new friends. You'll need them in this part of the city," said a cheerful voice behind her.

The boy! Emma swung around, heart hammering, as her captor popped up from the manhole. He slid the cover back and smiled jauntily at her. "Well, it's been fun. Take care!"

"What?" Emma stared, astonished, as the boy

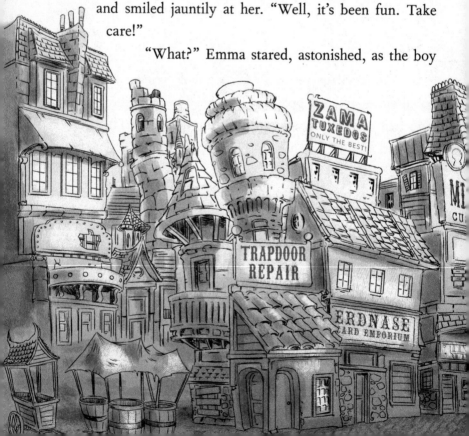

turned his back on her and sauntered away into the crowd. Within minutes he was lost to her sight.

She stood, shocked into stillness, as people shoved past her. The boy wasn't trying to kidnap her? He didn't care about her anymore? He was just going to . . . leave her here?

"Hey!" she shouted, and plunged forward, shoving her way behind two women, one carrying a shopping bag and one trying to keep a live chicken tucked under her arm. "Wait a minute!"

A block later, she caught up to the boy just as he was handing a pile of coins to an old woman in a patchwork jacket. The old woman nodded and stuffed the coins into her pocket before limping away.

"You again?" The boy grinned at Emma. He had dark stringy hair that he brushed from his fore-head, and his clothes were like those she

could see on all the people here—patched, worn, and faded. "From the minute I met you, you kept shouting about getting away from me!" the boy told her. "And now you're following me?" He sighed. "Look, I get it. I'm not trying to be charming. It just happens. Still, do your best to resist." He shrugged and spun off, slipping between the pedestrians with ease.

Infuriated, Emma ignored complaints from all sides as she pushed after him. "You can't kidnap someone and then leave them in a strange place!" she told him.

"I can and I did," the boy pointed out. In one hand he held out a gleaming diamond necklace. A little girl darted past, a blur of black braids flowing from under a tweed cap. She took the necklace and was gone.

That gave Emma an idea.

Quickly, before he could slip away again, Emma reached into the pocket of the boy's jacket and seized hold of whatever she could grab. Her hand came out full of thin gold coins, with a slender silver chain trailing between two fingers.

"Hey, no fair!" The boy snatched at Emma's hand. Emma pulled away. "Give it back!"

"After you bring me to the Tower," Emma said firmly.

"Hand it over," the boy insisted. "This is not the place you want to draw attention to yourself."

He made another attempt to grab Emma's hand. She slipped to the side with ease. After all, she had years of practice holding things just out of reach of her little brother. "Then take me to the Tower," she repeated.

"Keep your voice down." The boy cast a nervous glance

to either side. "Just mentioning the Tower around here can get you killed."

He was probably telling the truth about that, Emma thought. She noticed that the passersby were no longer pushing past as if she didn't exist. Instead they were clearly listening. Some were slowing down to take in every word. And by the looks on their faces, they did not care for what they were hearing.

Swallowing hard, she summoned the loudest voice she could. "DOES THAT MEAN YOU'LL TAKE ME TO THE TOW—"

"Shut up!" the boy shouted. "Okay! You win!"

"Good." Emma smiled and shoved her hand, with its treasure, deep into a pocket. "And you'll get this back when we get to the—" She cut off as his eyes widened with alarm. "When we get there. Deal?"

The boy groaned. "Look, I really can't take you to . . . that place. Really."

Emma raised her voice again. "That place? Do you mean—"

"I'll take you to someone who can help!" the boy interrupted. "Best I can do, I swear. Deal?"

Emma hesitated, and then nodded.

"And your name," she added. "You can tell me your name."

"I already did. It's Savachia," the boy said grumpily. "Come on."

He led the way. Emma followed, keeping her hand in her

pocket, making sure her treasure was safe. Halfway down the block, she saw Savachia's back stiffen. Then her gaze moved down the block, and she caught sight of three guards in gray—Tower guards—rounding a corner ahead.

Emma could have waved to them, could have shouted for help, could have run toward them. After all, she wanted to go to the Tower, didn't she? Pimawa had been taking them there. That was where she'd find Alex, she was sure. Christopher Agglar was there, and Agglar was supposed to keep both her and her brother safe.

But when Savachia darted across the road and down an alleyway with soot-stained walls, fast as a rabbit heading for its burrow, Emma followed him. Partly it was instinct—he ran; she chased.

But even more than that, the looks on the guards' faces scared her. She'd get to the Tower, all right—but she'd do it her own way. Not with them!

Just as they entered the alley, she heard Savachia spit out a word she didn't recognize. From the sound of it, it was a curse.

Four more Tower guards were headed straight for them from the other end of the alley.

Savachia skidded to a halt right in front of Emma. She slammed into him. Impatiently, he shoved her back with one hand while, with the other, he tugged at a gate between two buildings.

He yanked it open and forced himself into an opening barely large enough for a kid his size. Emma was on his heels. Those guards were going to have a hard time fitting through there!

She heard them shouting behind her as she followed Savachia along a tunnel so narrow that her shoulders scraped the walls on either side. Then, one after the other, they stumbled out into a square lined with carts and stalls selling everything imaginable: cogs and gears, top hats and sunbonnets, turnips, tomatoes, bread, octopus tentacles on sticks, and stew from a cauldron over a fire. There was even a man sitting in a chair getting a shave, while others waited in line.

Three roads led into the square, and more angry-looking men in gray uniforms were pushing through the crowd along each one.

Emma and Savachia were trapped. The steaming smells wafting from the vendors' carts, mixed with the oppressive stink of moldy wood and stagnant puddles, made Emma's head woozy. She surprised herself by grabbing on to Savachia.

"What do we do?" she asked nervously.

The old woman with the patchwork coat whistled from the corner. In one quick movement, every owner of a cart shoved his or her vehicle a few feet forward. Suddenly the guards were blocked, on the outside of a ring of carts, while Savachia and Emma were in the center.

From underneath the cart selling sunbonnets rolled a pyramid-shaped cabinet as tall as Emma. It rattled across the cobblestones to the center of the square. The little girl with braided hair peeked out from behind and nodded to Savachia before rushing back to her cart.

"Problem solved," said Savachia. He opened a triangular door on the front of the cabinet. "Ladies first."

Emma hesitated. Her first impulse had been to run away

from the guards . . . but had that been wise? Should she really follow this boy? He'd kidnapped her, after all!

The guards were angrily muscling the carts out of their path. They'd be through at any minute.

"Really?" Savachia snapped impatiently. He grabbed Emma's arm, and before she could pull away, swung her through the door and into the cabinet. He jumped in after her, latching the door shut.

Outside, booted feet thundered across the cobblestones. Fists banged on the cabinet. "Get out here!" an angry voice ordered. "Open the door now or we'll hack it apart!"

"Un momento, please," Savachia called politely. Inside the cabinet, he wrapped his arms around Emma. His breath smelled of garlic and licorice. "Hold on," he whispered.

Emma was about to demand why when the floor vanished and they fell straight down.

One more trip through the sewers, one more ladder, one more manhole, and then Savachia was leading Emma along a deserted brick street toward a theater designed to look like a pharaoh's tomb. Two sphinxes, their cracked plaster revealing the metal frame underneath, flanked the entrance.

"Here we are," said Savachia grandly.

"Where, exactly?" Emma asked. She eyed the shabby theater doubtfully.

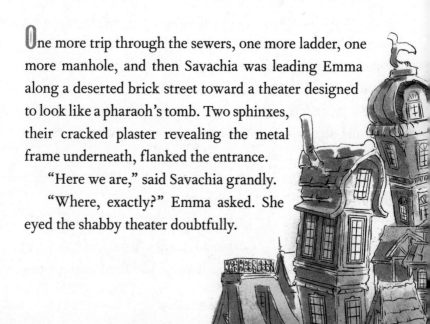

"At the Conjurian's premier palace of entertainment, of course!" Savachia waved a hand dramatically. "Home of the best magic shows in the world—in two worlds, really! Or it used to be, anyway. Before . . . well."

"Before magic started to fade away?" Emma asked.

"You got it. Come on. We don't want to hang around."

Yells came from the alley on their right. Glancing that way, Emma could see two burly figures holding a scrawny man up against the wall.

"Help me!" shouted the man.

She hesitated. Savachia shook his head and pushed her along the street toward the theater.

"Shouldn't we . . . do something?" asked Emma.

"Not our problem," said Savachia. "We have to go meet the boss."

ALEX

Alex looked down. Big mistake. It was a good thing that the cloud cover prevented him from seeing all the way to the ground.

Ten minutes ago, this had seemed like a very logical plan.

The Tower guards had locked him in a relatively comfortable room with a bed, a wardrobe, and a closet-sized bathroom. Fortunately, the wardrobe was full of extra bedsheets. Seven of those sheets, tied together, made a passable rope.

Honestly, he was a little embarrassed. Bedsheets! Climbing down a rope made of bedsheets was such a cliché. But it was also the most efficient way to reach his goal: the MAGE office, seven stories below.

The only thing he had not calculated was how long those seven stories would *feel*.

A gust swung him like a pendulum, back and forth, against the face of the Tower. Every instinct screamed at him to stop moving, to clamp his hands and legs around the sheet and wait for rescue.

But if he froze in place, either his hands would give out or the wind would carry him off. He could tell that his arms no

longer had the strength to get him back up the rope to the room he had left. His only chance was to keep going down.

Gritting his teeth, his eyes watering from the wind, Alex lowered himself until his toe scraped a ledge. A flock of bat-like creatures erupted from under the window pediment, flocking around him, their wings, velvety soft, brushing his face.

Instinctively Alex swung an arm to bat them away.

Bad mistake. Now he only had one hand on the twisted sheets, and one hand wasn't strong enough to hold his whole weight. It slipped. He flailed, trying to get his free hand back on the rope, but missed.

He fell.

Luckily the ledge was right below him, and it was a good wide one. He thudded down on it, his knees hitting first, then one shoulder. His body wanted to roll with the force of the fall, but he grabbed for any bit of stone he could hold with his fingers, clinging tightly.

Above him, his rope whipped in the wind.

Alex lay still, hugging the stone ledge, his heart thudding until he felt as if it might shake the entire Tower of Dedi. He never wanted to let go again, but he couldn't just lie here. Reluctantly, he peeled one hand away from the ledge and reached out to the window, only a few inches away. He tugged, trying to slide the window up.

It wouldn't budge.

Locked? It was locked? Why would anyone want to lock a window hundreds of feet above the ground? He made a fist and thumped on the glass in frustration.

The window swung inward.

Alex made a sound between a groan and a sigh and inched his way forward until he fell, headfirst, into the room.

He lay for a moment with his face in a dusty carpet, relishing the sure knowledge that, whatever happened next, it would not be a sudden plunge to his death. Then, still trembling a little, he got to his feet and closed the window, shutting out the wind.

He looked around to see where he was and flinched backward with a strangled yelp as someone loomed at him out of the dark. "I just—wanted to come in!" he blurted out, madly. "It was cold out there!"

Then he realized that he was talking to a mannequin. It was dressed in a long robe, and a heavy Egyptian headdress draped its bald head.

Past the mannequin, he could see a door with MAGE written backward across a rectangle of glass. As his heart settled down to a normal rhythm, Alex smiled. He'd calculated the correct floor—and better yet, he'd had the good luck to come in through exactly the right window!

There was a desk in this room with a chair behind it. In the walls were several other doors. One, he saw, had the names HENRY AND EVELYNNE MASKELYNE stenciled in gold and black across the polished wood.

His parents' names.

A sudden stab of feeling impaled Alex's heart. Was it hope? Fear? Simple surprise? He was honestly not sure.

Alex knew he should try to find Emma, and maybe Pimawa, too. Old Agglar, the traitor, had said that he'd have

Emma "shortly." Did that mean he already had her locked up in another room of this tower?

But that door had his parents' names on it. His parents, who were supposed to be harmless archaeologists, and who had *apparently* been something else entirely.

His parents, who'd been searching for the Eye of Dedi. That same Eye that everyone from old Agglar to the freaky Shadow Conjurer seemed to think that Alex and Emma knew about.

Maybe something on the other side of that door would explain things to Alex. Help him understand exactly what was going on here, and what all these people wanted with him and his sister.

He had to try to find out.

CHAPTER 8

ALEX

Alex opened the door with his parents' names written on it. He discovered a cramped office with shelves lining three of the walls, floor to ceiling. In the center, two desks sat facing each other, both buried under stacks of books, files, and loose papers.

In the midst of the clutter sat a framed photo of a little girl holding a baby. Emma, Alex realized. His sister, holding him, not long after he'd been born.

Everything was covered with a thick film of dust. Had nobody been in here since the day his parents died?

Died doing what? Not searching for old bits of pottery from the Nile Valley or lost Aztec temples, that was for sure.

Alex grabbed the topmost book on a pile. *Houdini's Lost Dove Act*, it was called.

"Probably a good reason it was lost," Alex muttered. He tossed the book gently aside, raising a cloud of dust, and grabbed the next, a small, slim volume called *Practical Magic Methods: How Not to Get Burned at the Stake* by Jermay Lucas. He flipped through the pages. Well, if he ever needed to switch two coins without touching them, the way Agglar had wanted him to, he'd found the right book to teach him.

Alex slid *Practical Magic Methods* inside his pants pocket. It would take him weeks to go through all the stuff on these desks, he realized, and he didn't have weeks. He probably didn't have many more minutes.

He took a quick look at the one wall that was not covered with shelves. Instead it had maps, photos, and small things tacked on with nails.

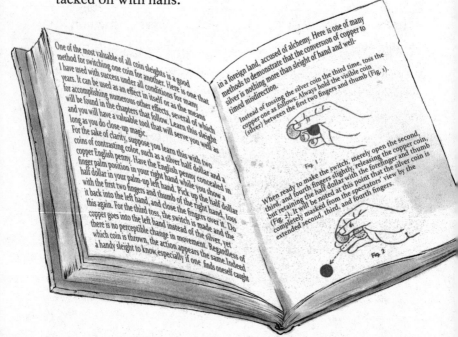

One of the most valuable of all coin sleights is a good method for switching one coin for another. Here is one that I have used with success under all conditions for many years. It can be used as an effect in itself or as the means for accomplishing numerous other effects, several of which will be found in the chapters that follow. Learn this sleight and you will have a valuable tool that will serve you well as long as you do close-up magic.

For the sake of clarity, suppose you learn this with two coins of contrasting color, such as a silver half dollar and a copper English penny. Have the English penny concealed in finger palm position in your right hand while you show a half dollar in your palm-up left hand. Pick up the half dollar with the first two fingers and thumb of the right hand, toss it back into the left hand, and close the fingers over it. Do this again. For the third toss, the switch is made and the copper goes into the left hand instead of the silver, yet there is no perceptible change in movement. Regardless of which coin is thrown, the action appears the same. Indeed a handy sleight to know, especially if one finds oneself caught

in a foreign land, accused of alchemy. Here is one of many methods to demonstrate that the conversion of copper to silver is nothing more than sleight of hand and well-timed misdirection.

Instead of tossing the silver coin the third time, toss the copper one as follows: Always hold the visible coin (silver) between the first two fingers and thumb (Fig. 1).

Fig. 1

When ready to make the switch, merely open the second, third, and fourth fingers slightly, releasing the copper coin, but retaining the half dollar with the forefinger and thumb (Fig. 2). It will be noted at this point that the silver coin is completely masked from the spectators' view by the extended second, third, and fourth fingers.

Fig. 2

Outside the window, Alex's sheets whipped back and forth in the high wind, tossing light and shadow across the room. One photo on the wall caught Alex's attention. In it, a dog sat looking eagerly at the camera, seeming ready to wag its feathery tail. The flickering light made the black eyes seem to wink at Alex.

At the bottom of the photo was scrawled a name: Bartleby.

Alex reached out a finger to touch the picture, its corners turning up with age.

Bartleby? That couldn't be a coincidence. Alex had named his mechanical dog Bartleby. Nobody had suggested the name to him; it hadn't come out of a book he'd read or a movie he'd seen. It had just been there, in his head, and it had seemed so . . . right.

Had it seemed right because, somehow, he'd remembered his parents' dog? Emma had never told him about this dog. Uncle Mordo had never mentioned it. And yet . . . could the name have stayed in Alex's mind, all these years, just waiting?

He pulled the photo off the wall. Had he ever thrown balls for this dog to fetch? Had it watched over him as a baby while he slept?

The photo the paper had been printed on was splitting at one corner. As Alex stared at the image, his fingers pulled at the slit. The backing on the photo peeled away easily, and Alex felt another sheet of paper beneath it.

A handwritten note.

Dear Alex,

Someday you will go looking for answers. If you have found this, I'm sure you have a lot of questions. It also means we failed to keep you safe. I wish we could be there to tell you everything. Take your sister to Plomboria. She's a dreamer. Brave but too trusting. Keep her safe.

Go now. Trust your instincts. And know that everything we did was because we love you and your sister.

Love,
Mom

After a while, Alex became aware that he had not moved for several minutes. He was standing in a darkened office, holding a letter written years ago by a mother he could not remember.

He was startled to find tears on his cheeks. Impatiently he wiped them away. What was there to cry about? It was not as if he had known either of his parents. It wasn't even as if this letter was helpful. It told him something he already knew perfectly well—that Emma was a dreamer who needed him to keep her clued in to real life. And it added something completely mysterious. What the heck was Plomboria?

He pulled the book on magic tricks out of his pocket, slipped the letter inside, and replaced the book. That was it. Done. And he was done with this office, too. Time to get out of here and find his sister.

He left his parents' old office, shutting the door quietly behind him, and turned to the door labeled MAGE, ready to head out into the Tower. Then he saw a blurry figure looming on the other side of the door, getting larger and larger. Footsteps thumped on the floor of the hallway.

Alex froze, but it was too late. "He's in here!" a voice shouted. The door banged open. Light flooded the room, and Alex took a step back, squinting.

"Master Alex!" Pimawa exclaimed in relief. "You gave us a fright!"

Guards in gray uniforms crowded into the room behind the giant rabbit.

"Climbing out your window? What were you thinking? You might have been killed!" Pimawa exclaimed.

Alex glared at him. "I was thinking I should figure out what is going on around here. I was thinking I need to find Emma. I was thinking I should never have trusted Christopher Agglar—or you!"

Pimawa looked stricken, as if Alex had stabbed him. The guards pushed past the rabbit, and one grabbed hold of Alex's arm.

"Easy now," Pimawa protested weakly. "He's just a boy."

Another guard shoved Pimawa back. "Watch yourself, Jimjarian. Get downstairs to the duty master for your assignment."

"That boy *is* my assignment!" Pimawa objected.

"Not anymore," the man snapped. "The boy's on his way to the mentalist."

EMMA

Emma followed Savachia into the gutted theater. Inside, most of the seats had been ripped out, and the space seemed to have been converted into a ramshackle village built out of planks of wood and scraps of metal. Dingy faces peered out from torn sheets that served as curtains. Cots and mattresses lined the stage, and people lay on them, some sleeping, some keeping a wary eye on everything going on around them.

Emma glimpsed a lean figure sitting on the edge of a cot, and she gasped with relief. For the first time since she'd come

down the stairs of her uncle's mansion last night, she felt sure that everything would be all right.

Her uncle might be dead, she might have lost her brother, and a spectral, eyeless figure with a scarred face might be hunting her—but here was someone who'd help, just as Savachia had promised. Derren Fallow, sleeves rolled up, hair rumpled, was examining the bandaged arm of a boy not much younger than Alex.

"Derren!" Emma shouted. She pushed past Savachia and charged up to the stage.

Derren's head jerked up and she saw his eyes widen. He set the boy's arm gently down on the cot before he got up and hurried among the beds to the edge of the stage, where Emma was clambering up.

She flung herself into his arms, and he hugged her tightly. Then he gripped her shoulders and held her out at arm's length, as if he had to make sure who she really was. Shaking his head, he hugged her again.

"Praise Dedi," he murmured. "You're alive!"

Emma's cheeks burned. Derren regained his composure and pushed Emma away again, keeping one hand on her arm. "I heard about the attack. Mordo and the others—I'm sorry. How did you get out? How did you *find* me? And Alex? Where's Alex? Don't tell me—"

"Alex is okay. At least I think so," Emma said quickly. "Pimawa got us away from Uncle Mordo's and here, to the city." Emma scowled at Savachia. "That's when he kidnapped me."

Savachia picked up an empty bedpan and examined it closely, as if he found it fascinating.

Derren let go of Emma and turned to glower at Savachia. "Agglar's turning up the heat. He's using the Tower guard as his personal army. And you decide to add abduction to your résumé? You have to stop taking risks!"

Savachia shrugged. "Explain that to them," he said, nodding at the theater full of people, who appeared poor and frightened and desperate. "I'm the only one financing this place."

Emma looked at the boy, startled. *That* was what he was doing with all the stuff he'd stolen? Giving it to Derren and his allies to help the people here?

Derren shook his head, exasperated, but didn't argue further. "Go get something to eat. Put that"—Derren wagged a finger at Savachia's bulging pockets—"with the rest."

Savachia emptied the contents of his pockets into the bedpan. Several patients turned their heads as coins and jewelry and something that looked like an Easter egg covered with silver filigree clattered into the metal receptacle.

"I did my job. You put it away," Savachia said, turning on his heel. He sauntered backstage.

Derren sighed. "He's a good kid, if you get past all the bravado," he said, almost as if in apology.

Emma nodded. She dug a hand into her pocket, pulled out the coins and silver bracelet she'd snagged from Savachia earlier, and dumped them into the bedpan too.

Derren raised his eyebrows but didn't question her about why her pockets were full of stolen goods. "Where's Alex?" he asked instead.

Ever since Savachia had fallen out of the sky to grab hold of her, Emma's life had been so bewildering that she'd hardly had time to think about her brother. Now she remembered those grim-faced guards in gray uniforms who'd descended on the Grubians' carriage.

"Those guards took him to the Tower," she said, and panic gripped her. Years ago, her parents had vanished. Now Uncle Mordo was gone too. She could not bear it if Alex were taken away as well. "We have to go find him!" she told Derren.

"Whoa, whoa, whoa. Calm down," said Derren. "We can't just run off and storm the Tower."

"But—but—Alex!" Emma stammered. "We have to—"

"There are some things you should know first," Derren told her. He sighed and looked away from her, running a hand through his hair. "Trust me, Emma. And now, come with me."

He led her through the dark, cramped backstage area, opened a door, and took her up a narrow, filthy staircase. At the top, another door opened, and Emma found herself on the theater's balcony.

"So are you a doctor or something?" asked Emma, looking down at the stage with its rows of cots. The boy Derren had been helping wasn't the only one who was injured, she could see. Others looked sick, sleeping restlessly as if feverish.

Derren shook his head and chuckled, but without much humor. "No. It would come in handy, but there isn't a doctor alive that could save the Conjurian. Look down there. Tell me what you see."

Emma leaned over the railing, staring down. Injured people. Sick people. A mother sat on an upturned crate, trying to quiet a fussy baby. A toddler wearing nothing but a ragged shirt wandered up and down the aisles, as if looking for someone he could not find. People were sleeping on piles of rags, hunched over tiny stoves as if they could not get warm, or just sitting against the walls as if they could not think of a thing to do.

"It looks like . . . well . . ." Emma hesitated, not wanting to be rude.

"This is the death of a people. What's left of a once-proud society of magicians," said Derren grimly.

Three small children, two boys and a girl a year or so older, ran up behind him. They tugged on his shirt, holding out a scrap of paper. Derren took it and folded the paper into a butterfly. The butterfly fluttered above Derren's graceful hands, rested briefly on Emma's nose, and darted off. The kids, squealing joyfully, chased after it.

"That was amazing," Emma breathed. "That was magic. Actual magic!"

It was not that she didn't feel sorry for the people in the theater below. It was not that she couldn't see the pain and misery and hopelessness spread out before her.

But at the same time, her heart was beating quickly with something that, she had to admit, was pure joy.

Magic was real.

Emma had always known it.

She had never told anybody, definitely not Alex, but she had always believed that one day she'd step into a wardrobe and out into a snowy wood lit by a lamppost. Or that an owl would drop a letter down her chimney, telling her she'd been accepted into a school for witches and wizards. Or that a tornado would sweep her up and drop her, house and all, at the start of a yellow brick road.

Now it had happened at last. And if the magical world she'd come to was in trouble—well, that was part of the story too, wasn't it? It always was.

Derren managed a weary smile. Of course, magic wasn't as exciting to him as it was to Emma. She could understand that. But it didn't quench her delight.

"A bit of entertainment. That is all it is, I'm afraid. It's all I have to offer—a few beds and bandages and a trick or two to pass the time." His smile evaporated. "Our power has faded away. For centuries we did real magic but pretended we could not, as long as we were in the Flatworld—the world where you grew up, Emma. We used bits of thread or magnets or hidden mirrors to explain away our powers. We created secrets to hide the one true secret—that magic exists."

"But why?" Emma asked urgently. "Why not just tell people? Tell everybody?"

Derren shook his head at her. "To avoid the gallows, that's why! Or the fire! Emma, for centuries magicians were hanged or burned at the stake. You know that."

Emma remembered Neil and Clive and their puppet show. The little puppets, tossed one by one down the hole in the stage, never to return.

"But that doesn't happen anymore! Not now!" she protested.

"No, not now. Not often. But the mistrust is still there. And it hardly matters now if magicians want to hide their real abilities, because we have so little left to hide. We became so good at pretending to have no actual magic that we didn't notice it was declining. But our powers have faded until they are almost gone. No one knows why, and it's too late to figure it out. What little magic remains is only good for party tricks or turning scraps of paper into lifeless butterflies."

"But what about . . ." Emma hesitated. "That guy. The Shadow Conjurer. And those skeleton things he had with him. That looked like real magic to me."

Derren's mouth twisted sideways in an odd manner. "Yes. The Shadow Conjurer. No one knows who he is or where his power comes from. Quite mysterious. And of course alarming." But he didn't sound particularly anxious.

"What about the Circle?" asked Emma, remembering something Pimawa had said. "Aren't they in charge? Isn't it their job to stop somebody like the Shadow Conjurer? And to protect magic?"

Derren lifted an arched eyebrow. "The Circle? My sweet Emma. You sound just like your parents. Come."

Emma followed Derren up a rickety ladder into the rafters, disturbing a flock of striped birds. Balancing along the sagging beams, he led her to a large, round window set into the wall.

Derren leaned against the empty frame, which was several feet taller than him, looking out at the city. Emma joined him.

Below, she could see the square where Savachia had helped her get away from the Tower guards. She could see old buildings, half of them abandoned, with boarded-up windows and doors. She could smell the stench of rotten

vegetables, which drifted to her nose along with smoke from chimneys and small fires built on street corners.

"The Circle is concerned with nothing more than holding on to its power. You've seen the results," said Derren. "People used to trust the Tower guards. Now they're nothing but brutes. Christopher Agglar uses them as his own army. He arrests anyone who questions him. People can be dragged off to prison or have their homes destroyed for pretending to have magical powers, or for not having them anymore, or for any reason at all. Most people are so frightened of the Shadow Conjurer"—his mouth curled with distaste—"that they don't dare protest.

"Meanwhile, our people are suffering. This world runs on magic, Emma. Without it, we can't grow enough food. We can't keep our houses from falling down. And what does the Circle do about all that? Nothing!"

"But . . . you're doing something." Emma looked up at Derren anxiously. The feeling she'd had when she'd first seen him—that everything was going to be all right at last—was starting to drain away.

"All I'm doing is bandaging the wounds I helped to inflict," Derren said bitterly. "I was a member of the Circle for a long time. I should have stood against Agglar. I should have stopped what he was doing. But it's too late now." Derren sighed, looking down at the city, avoiding Emma's gaze. "And your parents—oh, Emma, they died trying to find the Eye of Dedi, in the hopes that it could save us. And I—I'm partly to blame."

"They . . . died?" Emma repeated, so softly she could barely hear herself.

"Emma." Derren turned to look at her. "You know this. You know it's true. Your parents are *not* coming back."

Emma dropped her eyes and stared out at the dilapidated city. Derren was not the first person to say that her parents were gone forever.

Uncle Mordo. Alex. Everyone had told her the same thing: Mom and Dad had died. It was sad. It was terrible. It was unfair. But it was true.

Emma had never believed it. Because no one had been able to tell her *how* they'd died. Had their car crashed? Had their airplane fallen out of the sky? Had they gotten sick, somewhere in a distant land, far away from a hospital? No one would say. It seemed that no one knew.

So Emma had not believed it. She'd waited and waited. But her parents had not returned. And now Derren, who'd always been kind to her . . . who'd made her feel safe in this strange new world . . . who was trying to help all these poor people . . . Derren was telling her the thing that she'd refused to hear for so many years.

"They're gone, Emma," Derren said. "I'm sorry. I'm so sorry, but they're dead. And I'm . . . I'm to blame. At least in part. It was my fault, what happened to them."

Perched on ancient rafters, high above a stage and a city, Emma clutched at the windowsill. She could feel a current of grief tugging at her, ready to pull her into a whirlpool. Ready to spin her down.

She'd fought the sadness for so long, but now, in the magic world she'd always dreamed of, it was about to swallow her up at last.

"Come with me, Emma," Derren said gently, and started off once more on a zigzag path along the rafters.

Numbly, Emma followed.

CHAPTER 9

EMMA

Emma felt as if she'd been walking after Derren for days when they arrived at a red door, set at a lopsided angle in the wall between two beams that held up the roof. Once he'd opened the door with a large iron key, Derren stepped to one side. He swept his arm, inviting Emma in.

The walls, lined with books, rose to a slanted ceiling. At the far end was a stone fireplace, with two crooked chairs and a tattered couch beside it.

"Welcome to my home," said Derren. "Please forgive the chill." He strode to the fireplace. With one wave of his hand, the logs were engulfed in flames. "I don't make it up here often these days."

"This is lovely," Emma said, automatically polite. She was hardly even aware of the words she'd spoken.

Derren caught her staring at the microwave perched on a beam in the corner.

"Please don't report me," he said with a smile. "I need as many time-saving devices as I can smuggle in."

"Do you prefer sugar or honey in your tea, miss?" said a crackly voice above Emma. With a gasp, she looked up at a red parrot wearing glasses and a bow tie.

"Geller," said Derren, "how many times have I told you not to startle our guests?"

"Zero, sir," said Geller. "We never have guests."

"Just put the kettle on, thank you."

Geller flew from the shelf and snagged a dented kettle off the stove. The bird swooped past Emma and landed on a spigot over a tin bucket that served as a sink.

"He does make excellent tea." Derren brushed the dust off a chair and offered the seat to Emma. "Please, sit."

As soon as she was settled, Derren retrieved a large leather-bound album from the shelves and placed it gently on Emma's lap. She opened it, and her heart seemed to cave in inside her chest.

She ran her fingers lightly over the pictures. Her hand was trembling.

In one photo, they were the archaeologists she had been told they were.

In another photo, they wore matching green costumes adorned with yellow jewels and orange sequins.

Below that, they were in work clothes, her father standing by a large glass tank. Her mother was sopping wet, presumably from being trapped inside. Frozen in a burst of laughter next to the tank was Derren.

"They were remarkable people," Derren said gently. He collapsed into the chair across from Emma with a sigh. "I don't suppose Mordo indulged in any tales of your parents."

"He told us they were archaeologists. That there had been some kind of accident . . . that they weren't coming home," said Emma. "I—I never believed him."

Never.

"He did not lie. Your parents were archaeologists," Derren told her. "They met at grad school and fell in love. Their lives changed forever when a wealthy benefactor recruited them for a very different kind of archaeology. Christopher Agglar enlisted them as agents of MAGE."

Never work with animals.

Promotional photo for the Egypt to

Fifth dig site.

Testing Evelynne's new
water tank illusion.

Emma's 3rd Birthday!

Emma's new brother arrived.

Rehearsal, Paris.

The day job.

Derren paused and took in a deep breath before continuing. "Your parents believed that by exploring the past, by uncovering these artifacts, they could find a way to revive magic."

Emma touched the tip of her finger to Derren's laughing face. How different he looked. She could not imagine the man before her laughing like this, as if no sadness existed in the world. "How do you know all this? Did you work for MAGE too?" she asked faintly.

Derren shifted in his seat. "I did, yes. But not as a field agent like your parents. I was a methodologist." He saw Emma's puzzled look and answered her question before she could ask it. "We were the ones who invented ways to duplicate magical tricks without using magic. Sleight of hand, trick cabinets, props, and smoke screens. All of that. We invented it all to keep our secrets safe."

Derren held out his empty hand, then closed it. "In the Flatworld, it hasn't always been safe to do real magic. If a

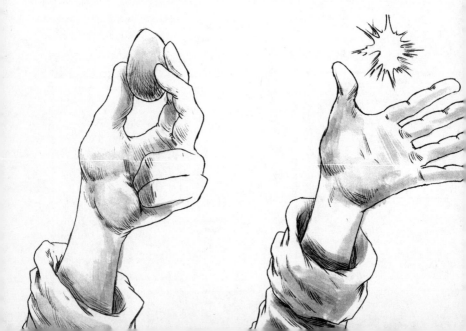

magician was hauled before the Inquisition or a Puritan judge or an angry king, methodologists like us were brought in to save them." He opened his hand, revealing a brown egg. "So to prove a magician was not in league with the devil"—he made a motion as if to toss the egg into the air, and it vanished before Emma's eyes—"the accused simply revealed his secrets." He turned his hand around, exposing the egg dangling from a thin string looped around his thumb. "Secrets to hide secrets."

Derren rapped the egg on the table, and Emma realized that it was made of wood. Once more he tossed it up, and the egg transformed into a dove that fluttered up toward the ceiling.

"I designed all the effects for your parents' show. We traveled the world together, performing everywhere—London, Sydney, Paris, Istanbul, Cairo, Tokyo. All the time they were on the track of Conjurian artifacts, recovering them wherever they'd been lost. But the Eye of Dedi was always our main target. We were Indiana Jones with a deck of trick cards."

Emma lifted her gaze from the old photographs. The Eye of Dedi. Neil and Clive Grubian's puppet show flashed through her mind. The magical artifact had created this world and trapped Dedi's magic, but this refuge for magicians wasn't a refuge any longer.

"They found it, didn't they?" she whispered.

Derren looked away from her, toward the fire. "Yes," he said simply. "Or so I was told. I wasn't with them at the dig site."

The dove swooped down onto Derren's shoulder. "I was in my shop, building a new chamber for your mother's water escape," he said, still staring into the fire as if he could see something there that was invisible to Emma. "Agglar burst in, in a rage. Not unusual for him, of course. But this time I knew something really was wrong. He said we were shutting down. Henry and Evelynne were gone. And he seized everything—all of your parents' belongings, all their props, every last thing. He took it all to the Tower. The show was over."

The dove cooed. Derren covered his face.

"Your tea, Miss Maskelyne," Geller announced. Using his beak, he pushed a cart between Emma and Derren.

Emma barely noticed him. She could not take her eyes off Derren. When she tried to speak, she found that her mouth was too dry, her lips stiff. "How—" she croaked, and she had to stop and swallow. "How did they die?"

"The official MAGE report stated that the dig site had collapsed. Henry and Evelynne were buried alive. That was all I ever heard. The report was classified, and I could not find out more."

So now she knew. What Uncle Mordo had never been willing to say, what Alex had never known. Her parents had died, crushed under tons of dirt.

Her parents had died.

"I should have been there with them," Derren said angrily. He still did not look at Emma. "I might have been able to . . ."

His voice trailed away.

Emma listened to the silence, flipping through her parents' old tricks to steady her trembling hands. Even the flames seemed to crackle quietly among the logs.

She was waiting for tears to come. Waiting for herself to start crying. Maybe even screaming. Waiting for herself to get angry at Derren for not having saved her parents, at Uncle Mordo for not having told her what he knew, maybe even at Alex for having been right all these years.

But none of those feelings rose up inside her. Maybe she'd killed her grief by refusing to feel it for so long. She reached

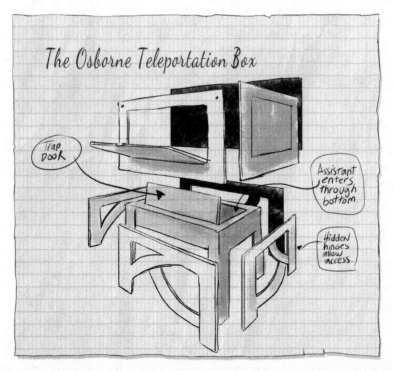

The Osborne Teleportation Box

Trap Door

Assistant enters through bottom.

Hidden hinges allow access.

out a hand, took a teacup from the parrot, and finally woke up her voice to answer Derren.

"It wasn't your fault," she said softly. "It was an accident."

Slowly, Derren turned to look at her. "You are kind, Emma. So much like your mother." He pushed the teacup away and rose stiffly, walking to the fireplace. "But it was my fault. And it wasn't an accident."

Emma took a swallow of tea. It was scalding hot, but it could not touch the chill growing inside her.

Derren shook his head. "I should've seen how it all fit together. I created tricks and puzzles and traps, but I couldn't see the trap we were all living in. It was Agglar! That warped egomaniac, willing to do anything to gain more power."

"Christopher Agglar?" Emma choked out. "You think he wanted—"

"He wanted the Eye of Dedi."

"To bring magic back?"

"Oh, Emma." Derren sighed. "No, not to bring magic back. Exactly the opposite, in fact. He wanted the stone—he still wants the stone—but not to save the Conjurian. He wants to hide it away forever. As the belief in Dedi fades and magic slowly dies, Agglar gathers more and more power to himself." Derren laid an arm against the mantelpiece and rested his forehead on it.

"So he killed my parents and took the Eye of Dedi?" There, she had said it out loud. Her parents were dead. But not in a car wreck, not in a plane crash, not sick somewhere far from home.

And not by accident, either.

Her parents had been murdered by her uncle's old friend.

Derren spun around so fast, Emma shot back in her chair, spilling her tea.

"Agglar killed your parents. He used MAGE as a weapon. But he didn't get the stone, Emma. He didn't get the Eye of Dedi."

"He—he didn't?"

"Henry and Evelynne were too clever for him." Derren's eyes gleamed with a savage triumph. "They hid the Eye. By the time he realized what they'd done, your parents were gone. And so was the stone. For some reason, Agglar believes you and your brother have clues to its location. That's why he came after you, last night, at your uncle's mansion."

"But—he didn't come after us," Emma protested, remembering the hall of Uncle Mordo's mansion, the door slamming open, and that horrible figure with the floating skeletons behind him. "It wasn't Agglar. It was—"

Derren spread his arms theatrically. "Right, it was the infamous Shadow Conjurer." He hunched his shoulders and made his eyes menacing. "Funny how this Shadow Conjurer suddenly appeared just at the same time the good people of this world began to lose confidence in the Circle. But if everyone is scared stiff that there's a blue-faced bogeyman behind every door—well, *then* people need the Circle. They need Christopher Agglar."

Derren knelt in front of Emma. "I know about tricks, Emma. And the Shadow Conjurer is a trick performed by a master of misdirection. You see, no one needs Agglar's protection if there is nothing to protect them from."

"You think . . . Agglar is the Shadow Conjurer?" Emma's mind was spinning. "And he—he killed my parents? And Uncle Mordo? But he has Alex! Right now!"

Derren dropped heavily back into his chair and nodded. "He'll come for you next. If he doesn't get what he needs from Alex," he said.

Emma shuddered. She'd been so close to heading for the Tower, putting herself in Agglar's hands! She'd very nearly made Savachia bring her there. Thank goodness he'd brought her to this theater instead. To Derren. To somewhere safe.

"And that, I'm sorry to say, is why you can't stay here," Derren told her.

Emma's mouth opened, but she had no breath to speak.

"I'm sure Agglar's goons are already scouring the city for you. And this place will be high on their list. I can't put all the people here at risk."

Emma felt as if Derren had punched her in the stomach. She wanted to double over in her chair.

Derren looked away, as if he couldn't bear watching her.

"Where am I supposed to go?" Emma asked when he said nothing more.

Derren shrugged.

"I'm sorry, Emma. I'm in no position to help. This city gets more dangerous by the day." He folded his hands on his lap. "Your only chance is to turn yourself in. Go to the Tower. At least then you'll be with your brother."

Emma sat very still, letting Derren's words sink in. Then

she pried a photo of her parents from the withered album and stood. "Thanks for all your help."

She wanted her words to be loud and to sting. They failed on both counts. Wiping tears from her eyes with one hand, she slid the photo into her pocket with the other.

Turning on her heel, she headed for the door.

"More tea, miss?" Geller cawed. She ignored him.

Turn herself in? Hand herself over to the man who'd killed her parents? Who was holding her brother prisoner? Of course not. She wasn't going to do that.

And she wasn't going to hide, either.

She was going to do . . . something.

She had no idea what.

All she knew was that she needed help.

CHAPTER 10

EMMA

As far as Emma could tell, Derren made no attempt to follow her as she wobbled her way across ancient beams and rusty catwalks to find a ladder that would take her down to the stage. Once she had her feet on firm ground again, she found Savachia's room behind the stage.

It was an old dressing room, with the boy's name carved into the door beneath the outline of a faded star. She knocked. Waited, then knocked harder. There was no answer, but the door swung open an inch at the impact of her fist.

"Hello?" Emma pushed the door. "Savachia?"

She checked behind her to be sure that the corridor was empty. It was. Then she nudged the door open wider. The room was not much bigger than the butler's pantry at Uncle Mordo's.

She slipped inside. A small cot had been wedged into place along the far wall. Near the end of the bed was a vanity with a cracked mirror. A photo of a woman with long black hair had been tucked into the frame. A few items were scattered on the table, including a deck of cards and a narrow metal box, open on one end with two leather straps attached.

Emma picked it up and turned it end over end, finding no clues as to its purpose. If Alex had been here, he'd have known in seconds what this contraption was supposed to do.

"It's my take on Devant's snowstorm. You know—you saw me do it when those Tower guards were about to grab me," said a voice from the doorway. Emma looked up to see Savachia leaning on the frame. "For being one of the greatest magicians of all time, kind of sad Devant only used that snowstorm trick to produce penguins on stage. It's a handy diversion and has so many applications."

"Good for kidnapping, too," said Emma, quickly replacing the box.

"That too," agreed Savachia. Letting the door shut behind him, he reached around Emma and scooped up the snowstorm device.

He opened a compartment on the metal box, revealing

tightly packed white pellets that looked a bit like pills. "Each one can create a blizzard. This fan part up here shreds the pellets and shoots out the flakes. Were you planning on swiping it?"

"I'm not a thief."

"Well, I am. So what do you want? Hurry up. I need to get some sleep before I go to work tonight."

"What's on the to-do list? Robbery or kidnapping?" Emma asked.

Savachia swung the door open. "I'm sure you can see yourself out."

"Wait. Sorry. I didn't mean to call you a thief. I mean, you're not a crook, you're—"

"A thief. Like I said. It's okay. I know."

"Why did you kidnap me?" asked Emma.

"You were in the right place at the wrong time," said Savachia. "Sorry, no special reason. I needed a diversion. You were just the most convenient escape plan."

Emma glanced out at the hallway. Savachia rolled up his sleeve and strapped his snowstorm device onto his wrist.

"Look, once you've been here long enough, you learn that it's all about survival," said Savachia. "You do whatever you have to do to get by. Your first and only priority is yourself."

"You don't believe that," said Emma. "I know you don't. You're stealing to help all those people out there in the theater."

Savachia snorted. "You mean paying my rent? Derren lets me stay here as long as I make myself useful. It works, that's all. Like I said, you do what you have to."

Emma looked around her at the cramped little room. "This is where you live? All the time? I mean, don't you have a home to go to? Parents or somebody?"

Savachia rolled his sleeve down. "My dad was a con artist. Bolted when I was five. Mom's dead. Derren found me hustling the streets in Boston. Brought me here. So now I run some of my dad's old hustles, plus a few of my own. Doesn't matter what world I live in, I guess—I'm always going to be a con man."

"You don't have to be."

"Oh yeah?" Savachia smirked. Then he caught Emma's serious look. The smirk vanished. "What else could I be?"

"Someone who helps me rescue my brother."

Savachia snatched the deck of cards from the vanity table. He flipped them into the air and caught them with his other hand. "You're suggesting I should be a kidnapper? Again?"

"Rescuing is not kidnapping," said Emma.

"It also doesn't pay well." Savachia shook his head.

"You promised to get me into the Tower. You can at least be someone who keeps his word."

"No way, you're not catching me like that. I said I would bring you to someone who could help you. I did."

"But Derren's not going to help me! He says I can't stay here!" Emma's voice rose with frustration.

Savachia looked just the tiniest bit sorry for her. Then he shrugged. "Sorry about that. But I did what I promised. I brought you to somebody who could help you. If he doesn't want to . . . well, not my problem."

Emma let out a long, slow breath. This kid was infuriating! But getting angry with him wouldn't help. She tried a different approach. "Then think of it as helping yourself. I guess Christopher Agglar isn't your favorite person?"

Savachia scowled. "He's nobody's favorite person around here."

"So, saving my brother would hurt Agglar's plans," Emma coaxed.

Savachia tilted his head, a calculating look slipping into his eyes. "Why is your brother so important to Agglar?"

Emma hesitated, shifting nervously from foot to foot, which she was sure Savachia noticed. This kid was a liar, a thief, a crook, a con man. He'd said so himself. She couldn't trust him, and yet she had to trust somebody. There was no way she could rescue Alex all by herself. She didn't even know her way to the Tower from here.

"Listen," she said slowly. "My parents—"

A shout from the corridor outside the room cut off her words. Savachia's head jerked up, and the cards slipped from his hands to scatter on the floor.

More shouts piled on top of the first. Then the shouts turned into screams.

"Stay here!" Savachia ordered as he bolted from the room.

Emma waited five seconds before taking off after him.

She found Savachia backstage, with his eye to an opening on a dusty black curtain. She crowded up behind him so that she could see as well. He didn't shake her off.

"Where is she?" a voice boomed.

Above them, on the balcony, Sergeant Miller confronted Derren, pinning the magician with his back against the railing.

Emma could not hear what Derren answered. She stared, appalled, as more guards shoved through the doors and swept down the aisles, yanking aside sheets, kicking down plywood shelters. A few people tried to protest and were met by blows from gloved fists.

"Don't make me ask again," Sergeant Miller growled. He grabbed the front of Derren's shirt and pushed, bending him backward over the railing.

"Is there another way out?" Emma whispered to Savachia.

Savachia snorted. "No, of course not," he said, turning away from the curtain. "I like getting trapped by the authorities in dilapidated buildings." In a second he was halfway up a metal ladder.

"Wait for me!" Emma scrambled up after him. The ladder sagged under her weight, not designed to hold two people at once. But it held as they scrambled onto a catwalk above.

Savachia did not glance back at Emma once. He ran easily along the narrow metal walkway, stopped under a hatch in the ceiling, leaped, grabbed a support beam, popped the hatch open, and climbed out.

"Hey!" shouted Emma. "Don't leave me here!" She was under the hatch when she felt the walkway tremble beneath her feet. Two guards were clambering up the ladder.

She looked at the hatch above her. It was higher than she could reach. Savachia had swarmed up a metal support beam nearby, but Emma could not see how he'd done it. The thing had no handholds or footholds. And if she slipped, she'd fall to the stage below.

Surely it was better to be arrested than dead?

The first of the guards crawled onto the catwalk. The second was close behind him. The catwalk lurched under his weight, and Emma could not hold back a cry.

"Just stay there!" the first guard ordered her. He got awkwardly to his feet and began to walk toward her.

The second guard, grunting with the effort, clambered onto the catwalk too. And it sagged.

Emma heard a cable groan under the additional weight.

Then she heard it snap.

The catwalk under Emma's feet tilted suddenly to one side, like the deck of a ship in a storm. The two guards scrambled back toward the ladder, and Emma fell to her hands and knees. She snatched at a railing, praying that she would not slide off.

There were screams from below. People crowded off the stage. Emma heard a chilling twang as another cable snapped.

Savachia's head popped down through the hatch. He stretched out his arm toward her. "Are you coming or not? Jump!"

"What if I fall?"

"You'll probably scream and make a gross splattering sound. *Behind you!*"

Emma looked over her shoulder and gasped. One guard had made it to the safety of the ladder, but the other had apparently decided he was not going down without Emma. He was inching toward her along the lopsided catwalk, gripping the railing with one hand, reaching for her with the other.

Emma staggered to her feet and jumped as high as she possibly could as the last of the catwalk collapsed behind her.

Savachia's hand closed like a vise around her left wrist. Then his other arm came down to snag her right wrist as well. "Got you!" With a grunt of effort, he hoisted her onto the roof.

Emma lay facedown on the tiles. "So I guess you're helping me?" she gasped.

"I'll have my assistant clear my schedule," Savachia answered. "This way. We need to get out of sight, fast."

Skidding and sliding down the slope of the roof, Emma and Savachia made it to a rusted iron fire escape that clung to the side of the theater. From there they dropped down into a narrow alley. Savachia pulled Emma along a few feet and then took hold of the brick wall of a building that was opposite the theater. To Emma's astonishment, he yanked at the bricks and they moved.

A cloth had been painted to match the brick wall, she realized. Behind it was a metal grate covering the entrance to a passageway so narrow and dark Emma could only describe it as a tunnel.

Savachia yanked the grate open. "In you go!" He shoved Emma in before she could protest and followed, swinging the grate shut behind him. The curtain fell over them, and everything was dark.

"Careful not to step on the rats," Savachia said.

Emma told herself firmly that he was only kidding. Of course he was only kidding. There were no rats.

Definitely no rats!

"I can't see anything," she said. She could smell too much, though. The stench reminded her of a sandwich Alex had hidden under his bed and forgotten about for six weeks.

"Keep going," Savachia told her. "There's only one way to go, you can't get lost, and—"

The curtain was yanked away, and light flooded in. The grate swung open. An arm in a gray sleeve seized hold of Savachia, yanking him out of the tunnel and flinging him away.

A Tower guard stared into the opening, blocking most of the light. "Be right with you, miss," he said with a sneer.

His face vanished. She heard several sickening thumps. She could only imagine what was happening—the guard must have hit Savachia, knocking him to the ground. Was he unconscious now? Was he dead?

Emma knew she should try to help the boy. He'd helped her, after all. But what could she do alone, against one of those guards?

Her panicked breathing echoed off the walls close around her. A dark figure reappeared at the entrance to the tunnel, blocking the light. It stepped in after her.

ALEX

All eight walls of the octagonal room were lined with shelves and cases, each full of cards, pendants, and crystals. In the center was a table draped with a yellowed lace cloth. Large orb lanterns cast flickering shadows over the scene.

Alex, sitting at the table, was having a hard time taking his gaze away from the wooden box in the center of the table. A skeletal hand attached to the top held it shut.

The guards who'd found him in the MAGE office had tossed him in the room and told him to sit still, stay quiet, and wait until the mentalist arrived. Alex had read about mentalists while browsing the history books in Uncle Mordo's library. Sometimes they were called oracles, or fortune-tellers, or prophets. But every time, they ended up being full of bunk.

In a few cases, like that of Rasputin, they ended up dead. You tended to pay a steep price for hoodwinking.

The door slid open. A woman entered, dressed in a deep purple robe. A veil covered her entire head, completely obscuring her face.

"Hey," said Alex nervously. "Just so you know, I don't really believe in this stuff."

The woman didn't answer. Didn't greet him. Didn't vary her slow, steady steps as she approached the table.

"No offense," Alex said a little more loudly, "but it just isn't my scene, and I don't need my fortune told, so how about I—"

Still not answering, the woman sat in a chair across the table from Alex. She opened the carved wooden box and withdrew an envelope, placing it on the table.

"Name a color," she said.

Judging from her voice, Alex thought she was probably not much older than Emma. He had to admit that the veil was a nice, creepy touch. It was seriously unnerving to be talking

to someone he could not see, knowing all the time that she could see him perfectly well.

Still, no matter how good this "mentalist" was at stage-craft, it didn't mean Alex had to play along.

"Plaid," he said with a sneer.

The girl picked up the envelope and removed a card from inside. She held it up in front of Alex.

Looking at the shaky but unmistakable scrawl, Alex read: PLAID. There was no hiding his astonishment.

"Our connection has been established," said the girl. "I am Princess Tenyo. Cooperate and this will be painless. Mostly."

"Right," said Alex, doing his best to keep the surprise out of his voice. He had no idea how the trick had been done—but it *was* a trick. He was sure of that. There was no way this girl was reading his mind. "So, what if I'd said *red*?"

Tenyo nodded at the card. Alex turned it over. The word *red* had been written on the other side.

Alex dropped the card back on the table as if it had stung his fingers.

"I sense your skepticism," said Tenyo.

"It's not exactly hard to sense that," Alex muttered.

"Relax. I also sense your fear."

Alex sat straight in his chair. "I'm not afraid of you. Or your tricks."

"Fear for someone else," Tenyo said thoughtfully. "Your . . . sister."

Emma. This girl knew something about Emma! "Where is she? Is she here? Does Agglar have her, too?"

"I may be able to tell you where she is," Tenyo said, "if you let me in. We must explore, together. Your past. A time when your parents were still alive."

"Good luck with that." Alex shrugged. "I was two when they died." He looked down and flicked the card across the table.

"I see something shiny. Metallic," said Tenyo.

Alex crossed his arms, turning sideways to avoid looking at the veil, which shivered slightly with Tenyo's breath.

"This is something from where you grew up. A personal item. Something you made." Tenyo leaned forward slightly over the table.

"I'll take your word for it." Alex rocked the chair back on two legs. Let her say something about Emma, and he'd help her out. But until she did, he wasn't playing this game.

Tenyo's slim fingers reached toward Alex. "What I have said . . . it does not mean anything to you?"

"Aren't you supposed to tell me?" Alex demanded.

"You are not cooperating," said Tenyo. A hint of anger trembled in her voice.

"No kidding. And *you* are not reading my mind!" Alex let the front legs of his chair slam down hard on the floor.

The door slid open. Agglar stepped in behind Tenyo. He laid a hand on the back of her chair.

"He's blocking me," said Tenyo.

"Tenyo is one of the few remaining mentalists in the Conjurian who still have their powers," said Agglar sternly. "If you cooperate with her, we may find a clue to the Eye's location. And that will restore magic to our world. It is what your parents wanted. What they died for. Will you do nothing to help their vision come to pass?"

"I never knew my parents," Alex snapped. "I don't have a clue what they did with this Eye thing. If they ever had it."

Agglar rapped his cane on the floor. Two guards appeared in the doorway. "If you do not cooperate, Alex, I will employ other methods to make you more . . . compliant."

"Yeah? Like *her* methods?" Alex lunged forward and grabbed the envelope that had held the card with PLAID written on one side. He ran his finger along the inside and held it up to Agglar; it was smudged with grayish dirt and trembling very slightly. "Carbon paper. She scratched my answer through the envelope, and the carbon paper let her write it directly on the card." He grabbed the card itself and turned it over to the side that said *red*. "Ninety percent of people will say *red* when asked to name a color."

The card shook in his hand, but he didn't look away from Agglar. If the guy was going to toss him in some dark cell, he'd go down showing them he couldn't be fooled.

The wrinkles on Agglar's face sagged. Alex had never seen that expression on his face. Was Agglar about to have some sort of stroke? Or was he just furious?

But the old man, instead of yelling or collapsing, looked down at Tenyo as if his heart had been broken.

"How long?" asked Agglar.

Tenyo's veil fluttered. "Two years ago, my powers started

to fade," she said faintly. "They were completely gone within a month. I . . . I thought if I didn't admit it to anyone, if I kept trying, they might come back. I . . ."

"Go," said Agglar.

Tenyo stopped talking. Silently, she rose and picked up her wooden box, cradling it in her hands. She walked between the guards and disappeared through the doorway.

Agglar slowly straightened back up. Alex had almost begun to feel sorry for him, but his hatred quickly flared into new life at Agglar's next words. "No matter. I have found your sister. I am certain we can jog *her* memory without magical aid."

Alex shot up. His chair went over backward. "Take me to her!"

"She is on her way to the Tower. You will see her soon enough." Agglar marched out, jabbing his cane at the guards waiting outside. "Return the boy to his room. And do make sure he doesn't try to fly away again."

CHAPTER 11

EMMA

The guard behind Emma prodded her up the steps into the Tower of Dedi.

Emma knew about towers, castles, fortresses, and citadels. Every fantasy book she'd read had at least one. But none of her books had prepared her to see a stronghold built out of a colossal tree.

Such a place, she thought, should be teeming with dwarves pushing carts full of gems or perhaps inhabited by dryads in fluttering green robes. Instead the only thing she saw (once she was inside) was more gray-uniformed guards at attention around a tall, wooden box.

Bit of a letdown, she mused. On the bright side, Alex was in here somewhere.

She just wished she knew where.

The guard who'd brought her inside marched with her to the other side of the room and through a doorway. As they passed through the entryway, Emma read the words carved into the wooden door: CONJURIAN DETENTION CENTER. Underneath, in smaller letters, the door read: THE ONE PLACE NO MAGICIAN HAS EVER ESCAPED.

Without saying a word, the guard took her down a flight of stairs and along a corridor hewn from a root of the enormous tree, through an iron door, and at last into an earthen room. A heavyset man with pale skin and deeply shadowed eyes sat with his feet propped up on a desk that was a tree stump. The nameplate next to his shiny boots read WARDEN PETER J. TURNER.

He glared at them over the top of the latest issue of *Genie* magazine. "I specifically told Stanton that we are full," he growled. He lowered the magazine, eyeing Emma. "Besides,

she wouldn't last two seconds down here. Take her to the holding cells on the forty-third floor."

"Master Agglar wants her held here until he can deal with her. Personally," said the guard holding Emma's arm.

"Master Agglar's coming down here?" said the warden. He slipped the magazine under a stack of papers.

"Yes. And if he finds us standing around chitchatting . . ."

"Right, right." The warden stood, fumbling for his keys. "Let's get her locked up."

The warden led them through twisting, curving hallways lined with cells, grumbling the entire time. Emma shivered when she noticed eyes staring at her from the small, square opening in each door.

The warden stopped beside a door, flipped through the ring of keys until he found the right one, and used it to unlock the cell. "In you go, miss."

With a shove from the guard, Emma entered the dark compartment. "There's someone in here!" she called out, her voice quivering with alarm.

"What?" The warden pulled his baton from his belt and shoved his way past Emma. "That can't be. It was empty this morning. I don't see anyone—"

Emma darted out into the hall, slammed the door shut behind the warden, and turned the key quickly in the lock. She pulled the key ring out and, with a wink, tossed it over her shoulder.

The guard who had brought her to the Tower caught it deftly in midair.

"Hey!" yelled the warden. He banged his fists on the cell door. "What're you playing at? Open this door!"

"Hush," said Savachia, pushing his gray hat away from his face and grinning at Emma. "Or we'll ask if any one of these upstanding prisoners wants to be your roommate." He flung his hat at the door.

The warden flinched and shuffled back.

"Well done, Emma," said Savachia. "Truthfully, I thought you'd wimp out and I'd have to lock you in the cell with him."

"Truthfully," said Emma, "I didn't think your plan would work. Must have been tough impersonating someone who is supposed to enforce the law."

"Well, it was harder than knocking that guard out." Savachia jiggled the metal box strapped to his wrist, the one he had called his snowstorm. "This came in handy. And of course it wasn't too hard to get in here, considering that I *did* have the city's most wanted fugitive in my custody."

"Thank you." Emma smiled, then looked away quickly. "Let's find Alex."

"Right," Savachia agreed. "We don't have much time. You start down there and I'll go this way."

Emma nodded, and Savachia walked briskly off in one direction, leaving her to go the opposite way.

Emma sprinted from door to door, calling for her brother. Most of the responses were quite rude, some employing words Emma had never heard before. She kept expecting, kept hoping, that Alex's face would appear at one of the little square windows, that his eyes would light up to see her.

But it didn't happen. Door after door showed her scowling faces, leering faces, hopeless faces, but never Alex's face.

What if he wasn't here? Savachia had promised her that if Alex was a prisoner in the Tower, this was the place they should look. But maybe that was wrong. Maybe Agglar was keeping him locked up somewhere else. There was no way she could search this whole huge tower!

Although Savachia could probably come up with a plan for that. She smiled just a little. Maybe getting kidnapped had been a stroke of luck after all. . . .

"Found you!" Savachia yelled from far away down the corridor.

Emma pivoted so fast she slipped. Regaining her footing, she raced back. One cell door was open. Gasping for breath, she peered in. "Alex?"

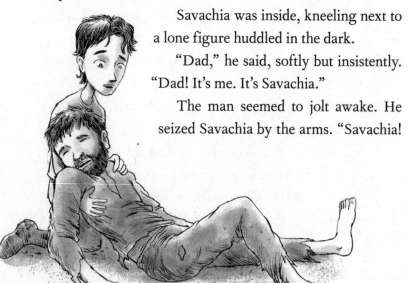

Savachia was inside, kneeling next to a lone figure huddled in the dark.

"Dad," he said, softly but insistently. "Dad! It's me. It's Savachia."

The man seemed to jolt awake. He seized Savachia by the arms. "Savachia!

It's really you! How did you . . . your mother . . . is she . . ."

"She's alive. Barely. We don't have much time. Can you walk?"

Emma jerked back instinctively. *Alive?* But before Emma could contemplate if Savachia was lying, the man nodded, tried to rise, and then slumped over.

"That would be a no," Savachia muttered. He wrapped his arms around his father's waist and hoisted the man over his shoulder like a bag of dirty laundry. Struggling under the weight, he got to his feet and staggered past Emma, out into the hallway. "Let's move," he told her.

"But . . ." Emma stared after him as he headed slowly down the hall, lurching under his father's weight with each step. "But . . . Savachia! What about Alex?"

Without looking back, Savachia said, "He's not here."

"You lied! You told me your parents were dead. You said you'd help me find my brother!"

"Technically, I . . . only said . . . my mom was dead," Savachia panted. He paused and raised his voice. "And I said I would help you break into the Tower. I never said I would find your brother. I'm sure he's in here somewhere." Grimly, he resumed walking, step after difficult step. "Keep looking," he said, barely glancing back as he tossed the keys to Emma. "Good luck."

He'd used her. He'd lied to her. The words he'd spoken back at the theater echoed in her mind: *You do whatever you have to do to get by. Your first and only priority is yourself.*

How could she have been so blind? She'd thought that she'd rescue her brother like a heroine in one of her books, and all she'd done was trust a thief and walk into a prison! A guard or another warden would find her soon, and she'd be locked up just like Alex.

Emma knew that she should run, hide, make a new plan . . . but all she wanted to do was flop down on the dirt floor and cry.

But that would mean that Savachia was right. That her first and only priority was herself.

And that wasn't true.

Her first priority had to be her little brother. He didn't know anything about magic. He wouldn't be able to figure out this strange world all by himself. She had to find him, help him. She could not give up now.

Emma pushed herself away from the cell that had contained Savachia's father. She peered into the next one. "Alex! Are you here?"

No answer.

ALEX

It was the same room as before. It had not changed . . . well, except for the iron bars over the window. And the fact that all the sheets were gone from the wardrobe. And from the bed as well.

Alex paced from one wall to the other, his hands deep in his pockets. As he thought, his fingers rubbed the surface of his father's old watch, the hands still frozen at a quarter past three.

He'd spent the last hour looking for a way out. He had tried loosening the bars on the window but had only a bloodied thumb to show for his efforts. He'd tried picking the lock on the door, but since he didn't have any lock picks and did not know how, that hadn't worked any better.

Never had Alex imagined he would miss his room back at Uncle Mordo's. But he did. He missed his tools. He missed Bartleby. He also missed the library, and more than anything he missed his dreamy, impractical, stubborn sister.

He not only missed her; he was worried about her. He knew perfectly well that Emma had always longed for a world like this. She'd spent half her life with her nose in books where magic was real. She'd never be able to keep her head now that she was actually in a place like this. She'd trust anyone. She'd believe anything.

She needed Alex to keep an eye on her.

So he had to get out of this room.

No tools? That wasn't true, Alex told himself. He still had his best tool: a brain.

And his brain had a tool that nobody in this world seemed to use: logic.

Alex paced faster, hoping the increased blood flow to his neurons would spark an idea. All right. He was in, apparently, a different world. That was bizarre . . . but the idea of multiple realities wasn't entirely unscientific.

This world seemed to be run by magic . . . but Alex didn't have to believe that, did he? What kind of magic had he actually seen?

He'd seen fish floating through mist and a kind of wolf-snake hybrid and a talking rabbit and an enormous tree. Pretty weird, but weren't scientists discovering new species all the time?

Big deal. Anybody with a cheap book on illusions could learn to do the same.

He'd seen Tenyo try to fake Agglar out and fail big-time.

And he'd heard an awful lot about the Eye of Dedi.

Alex slowed his pacing.

The Eye of Dedi. That might be the key. Was it some kind of magical amulet or artifact that could do miraculous things? Alex doubted it, but who cared? What mattered was that Christopher Agglar wanted it. Desperately. And Agglar was in charge around here.

Finding the Eye would give Alex the upper hand. Agglar would let him go and would hand Emma over if Alex could find the Eye and give it to him.

And the first step toward finding the Eye would be . . .

. . . getting out of this room. Which he couldn't do.

Great job, genius, Alex thought. *You just got all the way back to square one.* With a groan, he flopped onto the bare mattress of the bed and stared at the ceiling, waiting for another idea to come to him.

None did.

He stared at the ceiling some more. It was supremely uninteresting.

And the wardrobe in the corner was rattling.

Startled, Alex sat up, fixing his eyes on the piece of furniture. It remained still.

Okay. Nothing going on there. Probably just a change in air pressure making the wood shift in its joints like an old house creaking in the night. Nothing special. No reason to worry . . .

The wardrobe shuddered again, and its doors sprang open.

Alex rolled off the bed and dropped down behind it. Peering cautiously over the mattress, he saw that the wardrobe was empty except for a couple of wooden hangers rocking back and forth.

Okay. No reason to be spooked by a ratty old wardrobe. Alex stood up, brushing dust off his pants, and strode over and closed the doors.

The doors popped back open. Alex jumped away, tripped over his own feet, and landed hard on the floor.

"Master Alex?" Pimawa's head poked out between the wardrobe doors. A hanger was dangling from one ear. "There you are. Let's go!"

"You!" Alex jumped to his feet. His fists clenched. "I'm not going anywhere with you."

If not for Pimawa, he would not be back in this room. Or in the Tower at all!

"Please, Master Alex," Pimawa begged. "We need to find Emma."

"Agglar has her," said Alex. "Just what you wanted."

"She got away."

Hope flared inside Alex, but he squashed it down brutally. "I don't believe you," he said flatly. He couldn't trust the rabbit.

Pimawa stepped fully out of the wardrobe and lowered his voice. "There is much that you do not know."

Alex's eyes narrowed. "Yeah, people keep telling me that. That I don't know who my parents really were or what they really did. That I don't know where I am or how things work here. But you know what? I've learned a few things. That this

place is full of magicians who can barely do any magic, for one. That my parents died chasing a stupid relic for a madman who wants to rule the world. So I think I've learned enough."

"We don't have time for this right now," said Pimawa. "Please, Master Alex, you must come with me."

"Yeah, you said that before. And I ended up locked in this room. What makes you think I'm going to trust you now?"

"Because I was wrong," Pimawa answered. "Wrong about so many things. And I'm sorry."

Alex didn't have an answer to that.

"My first mission was to keep you safe," the rabbit said. "I thought that bringing you here to the Tower was the way to accomplish that. But I was . . . mistaken. Quite." Pimawa's large eyes pleaded with Alex. "I am still trying to keep you safe, Master Alex. I swear to you. But I would be happy to wait while you consider your other options."

Alex looked around the room and let out a long sigh.

He didn't trust Pimawa. The Jimjarian had turned him over to Agglar not just once, but twice.

On the other hand, escaping through a trick piece of furniture with a rabbit he did not trust was better than remaining locked up. With as menacing a scowl as Alex could manage, he nodded and followed Pimawa back inside the wardrobe.

CHAPTER 12

EMMA

"Alex!" Emma ran from cell to cell calling her brother's name. She would check every last inch of the jail if she had to. She was going to find her brother, no matter what it took.

Prisoners shouted back from behind every locked door.

"I'm Alex, over here."

"Let me out! I can be Alex!"

"Alex issssss in here, with meeeeee."

Emma paused to catch her breath, hands on her knees. Eventually the yelling died down. That made it easier to think. Sadly, the only thought that would come to her mind was how miserably she had failed.

"My, my, is that our dear Jane?" said a familiar voice from a cell nearby.

Emma's head jerked up.

"Neil?" she whispered. "Is that you?"

"Indeed it is, as I have not changed *my* name since our last meeting," said Neil Grubian. She could see his eyes now, peering at her from the small square window set into one of the cell doors. "As to the matter at hand . . ." His voice grew coaxing. "If, perchance, you could release us, we would surrender a rather valuable tidbit of information."

"Do you know . . . where Alex is?" Emma gasped. It was the only piece of information she cared about at that moment.

"Clive, is Master Alex, formerly Master Roger, in the library?" Neil called to his brother. "No? Well, then, check the solarium."

Emma straightened up.

"I'm not in the mood for jokes," she snapped. "Do you know where my brother is?"

Neil sighed. "Truthfully, no."

"Then goodbye." Emma headed off down the corridor toward the cells she had not yet checked.

"However!" Neil shouted at her back.

She paused.

"Given that you and your brother are, it seems, valuable commodities these days," Neil said, "finding him would be in our own self-interest."

Emma frowned, thinking hard. "Okay, then. So I let you out of there, and you help me find Alex?"

Neil grinned at her through the tiny window. "My dear, our new occupation seems to be nothing *but* helping you and your brother."

Slowly, Emma pulled out the warden's keys, fumbling through them until she found one that slid easily into the lock of the Grubians' cell. She hesitated. Could she trust two smugglers and criminals to keep their word?

She'd trusted Derren, and that hadn't worked. She'd trusted Savachia, and he'd let her down as well.

But she might be able to trust Clive and Neil. Not to help her because they cared about her, or because it was the right thing to do. But to help her because it would get them out of a jail cell.

Self-interest. Savachia had told her it was the only thing she could rely on. Maybe he'd been right.

Emma turned the key in the lock, hoping she wouldn't regret the decision.

The door swung open, and Neil bounded toward Emma

with open arms. "Good to see you again! How is your abduction going?"

She slipped out of his embrace as Clive ducked out of the cell and tipped his hat to her.

"Which way?" she asked them.

Neil cocked his head to one side. "My dear, don't *you* know? We haven't seen much of the premises, after all."

Emma looked from left to right. "Well, I've checked all the cells along there." She pointed right. "So I guess we can go that way. . . ." She pointed left, turned her head, and gasped.

Savachia, still supporting his half-conscious father, rounded a corner along the corridor to her right. He staggered in their direction at a lurching run.

"How adorable. You two are still together!" Neil

exclaimed. He held out his hand as Savachia approached. "Neil and Clive Grubian. Pleased to meet you, I think."

"We are *not* together," Emma snapped.

"Ah, quarreling already, I see," said Neil. "That happens a lot to couples who are brought together by kidnapping. Quite common. My, my. To be young and in—"

Emma yanked Neil's jacket, trying to tug him down the corridor. "Let's go. We have to find Alex."

"Not that way," Savachia huffed as he hurried past them. "It would seem the staff here have a strict no-escaping policy."

Emma gasped as another figure rounded the corner Savachia had just come around. The man stood there, glaring at all five of them.

"There's no way out," Sergeant Miller called. He strode forward into the passageway, followed by the warden and a squad of men. "Surrender peacefully and no one gets hurt . . . badly."

ALEX

"All clear," said Pimawa.

Alex crawled out of a hole in the wall where a secret panel had slid aside. The false bottom of the wardrobe had led them into a tunnel between the walls that had finally taken them here, into this white marbled hallway.

It was dotted with alcoves containing half-naked statues in poses that looked, Alex thought, horribly uncomfortable.

Pimawa tapped him on the shoulder and they were off, staying close to the walls.

"This part of the Tower was built by Heraclitus," said Pimawa in a low voice.

"He was a philosopher, not a magician," Alex muttered.

"Philosophy was his hobby, indeed," said Pimawa. "But he was a true magician, one of the greatest. He once demonstrated how he could move rocks with his mind. The ancient Greeks stoned him. There's some biting irony, wouldn't you say?"

"Can we save the morbid history lessons for another time?" Alex growled. Pimawa nodded and led Alex, in silence, to a spiral staircase that Alex found horribly familiar.

The two of them crouched down to peer at the main hallway of the Tower. It seemed as if weeks and weeks had passed, thought Alex, since he'd been marched through there in chains. There were still guards around the box in the middle of the room, plus more to either side of the doorway that led outside.

Alex groaned softly. "We'll never make it past all of those guards."

"As always, you are being much too practical, Master Alex." Pimawa shook his head, brushed the front of his jacket, and straightened his collar. "One thing I learned from Master Mordo is that belief can define truth."

"Was that from his lecture on how to become an eccentric recluse in three easy steps?" asked Alex.

"If we act like we are supposed to be walking out those

doors, no one will question us," Pimawa said patiently.

Alex shook his head. "That's a long way from a surefire plan."

"If you don't take risks, you will never achieve miracles." Pimawa thrust back his shoulders, puffing out his chest, and tugged Alex upright as well. He looked critically at Alex's posture and tapped his chin, so he held his chin high and looked Pimawa square in the eye. "I learned that from your uncle too."

"You can carve it on my tombstone," said Alex.

"Stop shaking," said Pimawa. "We are supposed to be here, remember?"

Alex shook his head again. "I'm not a good actor!"

"It's not acting if you believe it to be true. You have done nothing wrong, Master Alex, and neither have I. So you deserve to walk out the door, and I do as well." Pimawa took the lead and began to walk confidently down the steps, back straight, ears up, neither dawdling nor hurrying.

Alex followed, trying to keep his face expressionless, and hoping that nobody could see the sweat dripping down the back of his neck.

None of the guards

even looked up at them as they proceeded down the last flight of stairs. They walked right past the wooden box without so much as a second glance from the sentries.

This might work after all, Alex thought in amazement. *It might actually work!*

A guard stepped into their path.

The man locked eyes with Alex. Involuntarily, the boy shuffled half a pace backward. His feet wanted to turn and run back up the stairs, but what was the point? There'd be no escape, not with so many guards this close.

So he used every ounce of will to look as annoyed as possible, ignoring the panicky beating of his heart.

"Is there a problem?" he asked, doing his best to sound irritated.

"Your Jimjarian," said the guard. "Do you always let him walk in front of you?"

Was that . . . some kind of a trick question? What was he supposed to answer? Alex longed to glance at Pimawa, but he didn't dare. It would give the game away for sure if the man spotted him looking at a rabbit for instructions.

"Sorry," said Pimawa. He bowed his head and shuffled back several steps so that he was behind Alex. "I was a bit overzealous. Much too focused on our errand for Master Agglar."

"Speak only when spoken to," the guard snapped, narrowing his eyes at Pimawa. "Would Master Agglar really employ a messenger who can't keep his own Jimjarian in line?"

Oh. Oh! Alex knew what to do now. He turned to Pimawa and jabbed him in the chest with one finger. "Back in line . . . ah . . . Bartleby!" scolded Alex. "Speak out of turn once more and I'll turn your foot into a key chain!"

It wasn't like Pimawa didn't deserve a little scolding. But Alex still felt his stomach twist at the act. He didn't like his new role. He was acting as arrogant as his uncle, or even Christopher Agglar.

"Hmmm. Maybe there's hope for you yet," the guard said with a smirk. He turned back to his position near the wooden box and jerked his head toward the door.

"Well done," Pimawa said under his breath as he and

Alex moved on their way once more. "Quite convincing. Amazing what a little belief can do."

With a calm swagger and a new sense of purpose, Alex strode out the Tower entrance. No one stopped them. He headed down the stairs to the plain, where the tree roots rose in their twisted arches.

They'd done it! They'd made it! At the bottom of the stairs, Alex turned to Pimawa with a grin, holding up his hand for a congratulatory high five.

Pimawa didn't slap his palm. Didn't Jimjarians know about high fives? Puzzled, Alex tried to catch his eye, but Pimawa seemed to be staring at something over Alex's shoulder.

Alex turned and saw Pimawa's father, Rowlfin.

He was standing quite near the bottom of the staircase, in an archway formed of a tree root. A dozen guards in gray were at his back.

"Haven't you brought enough shame to our family name?" Rowlfin demanded.

"Father," said Pimawa. "Please, Father, you don't understand."

"Of course I don't," Rowlfin snapped. "How can I possibly understand why my son would betray not only his own master, but mine as well? Unless he has . . . plans of his own. Is that it?" Rowlfin advanced toward the steps. "You always questioned a life of servitude. I thought being chosen by one of the greatest magicians of all time would fix that."

"Father, it's not safe here," Pimawa pleaded. He put his paws on Alex's shoulders. "I believe Master Agglar is after the Eye for himself. Please, let us go. Master Mordo charged me with keeping the children safe. That is what I am doing. My duty to my master."

"He's right." Alex didn't love the idea of standing up for Pimawa, but the younger rabbit *was* right and his father was wrong. "Are you going to blindly follow Agglar, or are you going to open your eyes and see what's really going on?" he demanded.

"Enough!" Rowlfin shouted. He waved a paw at the guards. "Master Agglar will decide what is to be done with you!"

CHAPTER 13

ALEX

Rowlfin ushered Alex and Pimawa back into the circular room at the top of the Tower. With a groan, Alex flopped down onto the marble floor to ease his aching legs.

A burst of cold air chilled Alex's neck as the guards shut the doors behind them.

No chains this time, but what difference did that make? Alex knew he was a prisoner again, and no rope of bedsheets or trick wardrobe was going to get him out.

His parents' faces looked serenely down at him from their portrait on the wall. They weren't going to help either.

Once again, Christopher Agglar stood on the far side of the room. He'd glanced up when Alex and Pimawa were shoved in, and had then turned back to his window, looking down on the city.

But this time Agglar wasn't alone. Another man sat at the table.

"Derren?" Alex jumped up, new energy surging through him. "You've come to get us out of here!"

"Ah, Master Alex . . . ," Pimawa whispered warningly from behind Alex.

Derren smiled bitterly as he held up his cuffed wrists. "Afraid not, Alex."

Alex felt like falling back down on the floor. Giving up. Crying, even.

There was no way out, not this time.

"Quiet!" Agglar's voice boomed across the room. But he didn't turn around. He kept looking out the window, his back to them all. "I have dedicated my life to protecting this world, despite those who refuse to believe the threat facing our people. My job is to do whatever it takes to save what little magic we have left."

"Even if that means making yourself a dictator?" said Alex. No point in keeping his mouth shut now.

"If that is what it takes!" Agglar spun from the window, striking his cane on the table, inches from Derren's hands. "This man has done all he can to undermine my work. He has denied the threat facing our world. He has insisted that the Shadow Conjurer is a mere illusion! He has helped foster a rebellion among the citizens, encouraging them to question the leadership of the Circle. He fancies himself the Robin Hood of the Conjurian." Agglar's eyes narrowed, lips pulled tight against his teeth. "What has that gotten our people? What help has he given?"

Agglar turned his cold gaze on Alex. "Your sister came to him for help. For protection. He turned her away."

Alex stared at Derren. "Emma? You . . . didn't help her?" His stomach seemed to be falling all the way back to the first floor of the Tower. A lifetime ago, Alex had been sure that Derren would help them, no matter what.

Derren held up his bound hands. "I made sure she didn't end up like this," he answered.

"Silence." Agglar whacked his cane against Derren's chair this time. The younger man didn't flinch. "Master Alex, I will find her. I will find the Eye. You can stand by and watch this world break apart, or you can join me."

"I don't care what happens to this world!" Alex shouted. "I don't care what you want, or what you're doing, or anything! I just want to find my sister! I just want to go home!"

Home to a world he understood. Home where things might be hard, but at least they made sense.

Agglar put the tip of his cane back on the ground

and leaned on it with both hands, glaring at Alex. "What home, boy? Your uncle's empty house? If the Shadow Conjurer succeeds, there will be no home for anyone. Not here and not in the Flatworld, either. You need not like me. Only trust me."

"I don't think any of you even know what that word means," Alex spat. He looked from Derren, who'd abandoned his sister when she needed him, to Pimawa, who'd handed him over to his enemy, to Agglar. "Trust *you*? My parents trusted you so much they hid the Eye from you."

Agglar laughed, barely loud enough for Alex to hear. "So I always thought. What did you find in their office, boy? I will give you one opportunity to tell me."

Alex felt as if the note from his mother were about to burn a hole through his pocket, revealing itself to Agglar, to Derren, to everyone. He took half a step backward, as if that would protect him. He could feel Pimawa close behind him.

"Bravo," Derren muttered. He bent his wrists in, toward each other, and then out. "This is why your old stage show failed. You terrified the children." He gave his hands a shake and dangled the cuffs from one free hand. "Cheap theatrics. That's all you were ever about. Although, I must admit, this Shadow Conjurer of yours is an exquisite production. Should've put that in your old stage show instead of making tired elephants disappear."

The older magician whipped his cane up, stopping it a millimeter from Derren's throat. "I have wasted enough time on you," Agglar snarled.

"Master Agglar!" yelled Rowlfin, real panic in his voice.

Everybody looked up as the Jimjarian pointed out the window. Alex felt as if his throat and lungs were suddenly coated with ice.

One of the creatures he'd last seen in his uncle's house—a Rag-O-Roc—was gliding through the sky, skeletal white face gleaming, ragged black robes rippling in the wind. On its back was the man with the sickly blue face marked by three red scars. The Shadow Conjurer.

More Rag-O-Rocs thronged the skies behind him. All of them were soaring directly toward the Tower.

Agglar whipped away from Derren to plant himself at the window, feet braced on the floor. He wrenched his cane apart and slid a thin sword out of its interior. "Master Fallow, get the boy out of here!" he ordered.

Derren wasted no time.

He leaped up from his chair and vaulted over the table. As he slid over its surface, Alex, frozen with shock, watched the window explode. Shards of glass showered Agglar, who stood firm, unflinching.

A Rag-O-Roc swept in. Rowlfin leaped toward the creature as if to defend Agglar, but it thrust one bony arm at him and sent him sprawling to the floor. Outside the broken window, Alex could see the upright form of the Shadow Conjurer, standing casually on empty air, hundreds of feet above the ground.

Somehow that seemed odder than the flying skeleton that was now snarling at Agglar through bared teeth.

Derren landed on the other side of the table, feet away from Alex and Pimawa, as the Shadow Conjurer stepped calmly inside, flicking broken glass off his robe.

"So glad I didn't miss you this time, Christopher," the Shadow Conjurer said, and Derren swung around so that he faced the threat head-on. Alex stared at the Shadow Conjurer's face. The three red scars ran angrily down his face, and it almost seemed as if he could see perfectly well out of his featureless face.

"A sword? Really?" The bluish face wore a mocking leer. "Let me tell you from experience, it is a true pleasure to have enough power to not need such a barbaric weapon."

Rag-O-Rocs flooded in through the broken window in a torrent of black.

"Let's go!" Derren shouted. Turning back, he shoved Pimawa and Alex toward the exit. But Pimawa twisted away from Derren's hand.

"Father!" he yelled.

Turning his head, Alex saw that the Rag-O-Rocs had engulfed Agglar entirely. His sword flashed and then disappeared into a raging frenzy of black cloth and clanking bones. Rowlfin stumbled to his feet, staring at the place where he'd last seen his master.

Overhead, a wrenching sound startled Alex, and he jerked his head up as splinters of wood and a shower of plaster dust fell down upon him. A Rag-O-Roc's grinning face peered at him through a hole in the roof. Skeletal fingers pried at tiles and rafters, and more and more holes appeared.

A sucking wind began to tug at Alex's hair and his clothes, as if it wanted to waft him up within reach of the Rag-O-Rocs trying to tear the roof apart. Pimawa was staggering toward his father. Derren spat out a word Alex had only recently learned and lunged forward, grabbing the older Jimjarian by the collar and jerked him out of the way of a chair that suddenly swept up toward the disintegrating roof.

"Run!" Derren bellowed at Alex, but the rising wind snatched his voice away and Alex could barely hear him. "Move! Now!"

Alex moved. He, Derren, Pimawa, and Rowlfin raced for the door, fighting the wind. The Shadow Conjurer stood as still as a pillar, watching with a mocking smile on his distorted face.

EMMA

"That one!" Warden Turner strode down the corridor, pointing at Emma. "I have a special cell for her." He stopped a few feet away from Emma. The Grubians were right next to her, Savachia and his father a little behind.

Savachia let go of his father for a moment to thrust his arm over Emma's shoulder. Sergeant Miller jumped forward to grab the boy's wrist, yank up his sleeve, and remove the snowstorm device. "No squalls in the forecast today," he said, tossing the metal box away.

The ground vibrated under their feet. Dirt showered down from the ceiling.

"Earthquake!" came a panicked voice from one of the cells.

Sergeant Miller looked alarmed. Emma backed away from the sergeant—but where could she run that these men could not catch her?

More alarmed cries erupted from the other inmates.

"Quiet down!" yelled the warden. "We don't get earthquakes in the Conjurian."

The floor seemed to disagree. It lurched suddenly, throwing Emma to her knees. Several guards staggered. One or two fell.

"Hidey-ho, time to go!" Neil exclaimed. He nodded at Clive.

Clive grabbed his brother under one arm and Emma under the other and plowed past Sergeant Miller, knocking him into a wall. Before the sergeant could catch his balance again, Clive had barreled past the rest of the guards.

Squashed and breathless under Clive's enormous arm, Emma had only the vaguest sense of what was happening. Dirt fell on her head. A rock the size of her fist bounced off Clive's shoulder. There was shouting from behind her and from the cells on either side. She didn't know where Savachia was or what had happened to Sergeant Miller and his men. But she could tell which way Clive was going—and she knew it wasn't right.

"You're going the wrong way!" she shouted.

"Men of our stature never leave a prison by the front door," said Neil from under Clive's other arm. Then he whispered to his brother, "Are you sure it was this way?"

The whole prison shivered, and Clive staggered, nearly dropping his burden.

"Don't leave us in here!" cried a desperate voice from behind a cell door. "This place is coming down!"

Emma squirmed and twisted under Clive's arm. "We have to let them out!" she gasped.

"No time," Neil answered grimly. And this time he didn't add a joke.

Parts of the ceiling rained onto Emma's feet. She craned her neck to see behind her and caught sight of Savachia, dragging his father's limp body along the corridor.

Clive suddenly stopped as the most serious tremor yet shook the entire prison. He dropped to his knees, pulling Emma and Neil with him to the floor, shielding their bodies with his own.

Savachia, right behind them, tripped over Clive's feet and fell on top of their mound of bodies.

Emma heard a rumbling that grew into a muffled roar. She heard screams.

A wave of dirt rushed over her, sealing her inside pitch blackness.

ALEX

Alex sprinted down the spiral stairs of the Tower, jostled by panicked Conjurians fleeing alongside him. Derren and Pimawa and Rowlfin were somewhere in the chaos, but he didn't dare look back. One misstep and he would be trampled.

"Keep going!" he heard Derren shout from behind. "Whatever you do, don't stop!"

Around and around they went, spiral after spiral, until Alex was dizzy with more than terror. The building shook. The stairs trembled under his feet. In less time than he would have believed possible, he saw the main hall just one flight below.

The building gave a particularly bad lurch as he was more than halfway down, and he felt himself begin to lose his balance. He flexed his knees, shoved off, and jumped, landing hard on the floor, falling, tumbling, and colliding with a Jimjarian and then with a man in a plum-colored velvet tuxedo.

The rabbit bounded up without a word and raced on, while the man growled at Alex and staggered to his feet. Alex rolled over, got up, and headed out the door, ignoring his throbbing knees and the ache in his shoulder where he'd landed.

Derren had been right. Alex knew he couldn't stop. Whatever happened, he couldn't stop.

A car-sized chunk of stone thudded from the ceiling, crashing down to Alex's right. He dodged to the left and ran on. The door was just ahead of him, but it felt as if it were miles away. At last he stumbled through it and down the steps to the packed dirt of the field.

But it wasn't far enough.

If the whole Tower was about to fall—and it seemed very likely—then he had to get as far away from it as he could.

The Conjurians seemed to feel the same. He was caught up in a crowd, pushing forward, running, staggering, stumbling. All of them moving as fast as they could.

What about Emma? Was she back in that Tower somewhere? But Alex had no way to get to her. No way to find her. He could only hope that she was doing what he was doing—getting out. Getting away.

His foot caught on something and he lurched forward, hands out, to meet the ground. He knew, as he fell, how dangerous this was. He couldn't stay on the ground. He'd be trampled into jelly. He had to get up. Keep moving. Keep running . . .

A hand grabbed his collar and yanked him back to his feet.

"Don't stop!" Pimawa shouted in his ear, letting him go.

As if Alex needed a reminder.

The Jimjarian and the boy ran with the rest, ducking under arches made of mammoth tree roots. Alex could feel the roots straining and shaking. The Tower was pulling at its foundations as it swayed under the attack of the Rag-O-Rocs and the Shadow Conjurer. The poor roots could not hold it up much longer.

At last he and Pimawa made it across the field and into the first of the city streets. Pimawa pulled Alex into the doorway of a shop, and Alex collapsed, gasping, heaving in huge breaths.

They'd done it. They'd gotten out. They were safe.

The streets were packed. People were still streaming past,

away from the Tower. "Should we . . . keep going?" Alex wheezed.

Pimawa pointed back the way they'd come.

Alex stared as a dust cloud rose up into the sky, billowing larger by the second. It came from the field where the Tower stood.

Where the Tower used to stand, Alex realized. It was gone.

Emma. Had Emma still been inside when it fell?

"Master Fallow!" Pimawa croaked out. "Father!"

Derren was stumbling down the street with Rowlfin a step behind. The two joined Alex and Pimawa in their doorway, watching the dust rise and the citizens of the city panic.

"We have to keep going," Derren said firmly.

"We're safe here," Pimawa said, putting a gentle paw on Alex's shoulder. "We're far enough away."

"Not from them," Alex said. He pointed up into the sky, at the tattered black forms sailing toward them.

CHAPTER 14

ALEX

Running away from flying creatures, Alex thought grimly, was pretty much completely pointless.

It didn't matter which way the four of them ran; the Rag-O-Rocs, soaring overhead, kept pace easily. Every now and then they swooped so low that the hem of a tattered robe or a trailing sleeve brushed the top of Alex's head. But they never grabbed him. They seemed to be . . . waiting for something.

Alex didn't want to imagine what that could be.

"In here!" Derren shouted. He waved them over to a vacant shop. Above the door, a giant glowing sign showed a deck of cards, slowly rotating.

Alex dashed across the street and tore inside the shop. Derren was right—they had to get off the streets.

But the Rag-O-Rocs, apparently, did not want them to.

Rowlfin and Pimawa had barely followed Alex inside when a Rag-O-Roc crashed through the front window. Its bony hands were reaching out like the claws of a hunting bird, straight for Alex.

"We can't get trapped in here! Out! Out!" Derren ordered. He seized Alex's shoulder and shoved him toward the door.

Broken glass crunched under Alex's sneakers as he raced back through the door and onto the street once more. Another Rag-O-Roc dove at him. He ducked. The creature swerved up and smashed into the neon sign. Red and blue sparks showered down.

The Rag-O-Roc seemed to have gotten stuck in the neon tubes somehow; it hissed and struggled above Alex's head. But the one inside the shop soared right back out the broken window as Derren, Pimawa, and Rowlfin followed Alex out the door.

They ran. Again. Each breath hurt Alex's chest, and his heart pounded at his ribs like it wanted to escape. He couldn't keep this up much longer; he knew it. But he couldn't stop. Couldn't rest. Couldn't even slow down.

He was helpless.

No, he told himself angrily as he skidded around a corner after Derren. No. He couldn't fight the Rag-O-Rocs off. He'd seen what had happened to Agglar when *he'd* tried it.

There would be time later (Alex hoped) to admit how wrong he'd been about Agglar. The man might have been a power-mad tyrant—but he wasn't a villain. He'd died doing his best to protect Alex from the Shadow Conjurer.

Now Alex had to protect himself.

He had no weapons, true. But weapons hadn't saved Agglar. The man's sword had been useless.

However, Alex had something that was better than a sword.

His mind.

He needed a strategy, that was all. Something better than running because he was being chased.

Derren turned suddenly to race down a narrow alley between two buildings. Alex ran after him, but he felt himself slowing. Gasping for air. Thinking.

To defeat his enemies, he had to understand them. He had to think about how *they* were thinking.

Why were these things chasing him? What did they want?

They wanted him, Alex. Okay, obvious. But also interesting.

They wanted him, not Agglar. Not Derren. Not Pimawa or Rowlfin or anyone else, apparently, in the entire city.

If all they cared about was Alex . . . then Alex could use that fact to his advantage.

They spilled out of the alleyway onto a cobblestone street. Alex quickly looked both ways. To the right, the street went uphill, with shops to one side and narrow houses on the other. To the left, downhill, Alex caught a glimpse of the river, which would eventually run to the Sea of Dedi.

"Go right!" he yelled to Derren. "That way! It's better!"

As Derren turned right, a Rag-O-Roc swept down on him. Derren dropped to the pavement and flipped. Pimawa jumped to one side, careening into Rowlfin, nearly knocking his father down.

Alex dodged left.

"Find Emma! Take care of her!" he shouted with as much breath as he had left.

And he ran.

At least going left meant he was going downhill. That helped. A little. He heard Pimawa shout, "Master Alex! Wait!" He heard a wordless roar from Derren—anger? Disapproval? Fear?

It didn't matter. Alex didn't stop. He kept running.

The Rag-O-Rocs swarmed after him like wasps. Angry wasps. Angry skeleton wasps. So his plan was working! He'd lured the monsters away from Derren and the others. That would give them time to find Emma and get her out of here.

If Emma hadn't been buried under tons of wood and rock as the Tower collapsed, of course.

But Alex had gotten out. He'd been at the very top, and he'd gotten out. So had Derren and Pimawa and Rowlfin.

He had to believe that Emma had done the same.

The street narrowed as he ran. The Rag-O-Rocs, packed in a tight bunch, soared overhead. They didn't swoop down to grab him, though. And that was odd. It was almost as if they *wanted* him to go this way. . . .

Well, yes. Maybe they did.

Because this street had led Alex right into a dead end.

He slowed. He stopped. Ahead of him the road sloped down to the muddy gray river. On either side, buildings stood shoulder to shoulder. No alleys. No other roads. Nowhere else to run.

The flock of Rag-O-Rocs overhead began to sink lower. They did it slowly. They were in no hurry now.

Where the road met the water, an ancient dock jutted out into the river. Alex glanced up and heaved himself into a run once more, as fast as his quivering legs would take him. In a moment his feet were thudding on the old wooden boards of the dock.

Underneath, water sloshed and gurgled against thick wooden pilings.

When he got to the end of the dock, Alex didn't break his

stride. He dove straight into the murky water, feeling it close over his head with a cold shock that felt almost as if a Rag-O-Roc had grabbed him.

Maybe Rag-O-Rocs didn't like water. He had to hope so, anyway. It was his last chance.

Beneath the water, Alex twisted to look up at the surface. He blinked his eyes open and watched the hazy black forms of the Rag-O-Rocs fluttering above the water.

What do you know? He'd guessed right. It looked like Rag-O-Rocs couldn't swim.

It was a pity that Alex couldn't either.

As he sank deeper, he couldn't help thinking he could have used fewer visits to the library and more to the pool.

But that was about all he had time for.

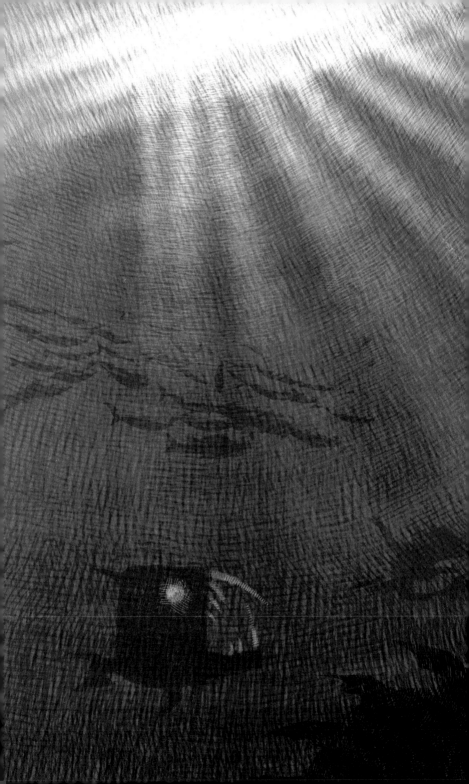

Acknowledgments

These books would not have happened without my own Magic Circle: my wife, Tammy; Rosemary Stimola; Phoebe Yeh; April Ward; Elizabeth Stranahan; and Sarah Thomson. Thank you for always believing.

ABOUT THE AUTHOR

Brian Anderson is the creator of the syndicated comic strip *Dog Eat Doug,* which enjoys an international fan base both on and offline. He is an optioned screenwriter and the author of several children's books, including *Nighty Night, Sleepy Sleeps; The Prince's New Pet;* and *Monster Chefs.* Brian's uncle was a charter member of the Magic Castle and taught him his first card trick in second grade. He has been practicing magic ever since.

Don't let the magic end.
Turn the page for a sneak peek at
The Conjurers #2: *Hunt for the Lost*!

COMING SPRING 2021!

CHAPTER 1

EMMA

I'm blind, thought Emma, instinctively rubbing her eyes. She opened and closed them

No difference. This was not good.

She detected damp earth, tasting it, crunching it between her teeth. Every breath scratched her throat.

She tried calling to the others, but no sound escaped her grime-coated mouth.

I'm buried alive!

Panic crept through her. What had happened? She remembered Clive Grubian picking her up and carrying her under one enormous arm—his brother, Neil, under the other—as the Conjurian Detention Center shook around them. The boy, Savachia, had been behind them, dragging his father. Then Clive had let her fall and collapsed on top of her, a second before a wave of dirt exploded down the corridor, destroying all light and sound.

Clive had saved her. If you counted being buried alive as safe. But she couldn't see. She couldn't move.

And what about her brother? What about Alex?

She'd bluffed her way into this prison to find and rescue Alex. But she hadn't been able to locate him. Had he been locked in one of the cells? Had he been crushed when the earthquake hit?

Did that mean Emma had been left all alone? No family at all?

Something grunted and moved above her, and suddenly Emma could breathe more easily. A hand seized her arm and pulled her up through a few inches of loose dirt, and she was standing in the corridor, coughing and gasping.

"Neil? Clive?" she sputtered.

"I hope they're crushed under the debris," muttered an irritated voice—Savachia's. He coughed. "Some help they turned out to be."

"Neil!" Emma called again, ignoring the boy.

Sparks flickered in front of her eyes. Then Neil's face, round as the moon, appeared in front of her, lit by a flame dancing on the tip of his thumb.

"You're alive!" Emma beamed with relief. She barely knew the two Grubian brothers, but in the relief of knowing that she was not all alone in the dark, she could have hugged the short, rotund Neil and his gigantic brother, Clive, visible now as the flame on Neil's thumb grew bigger and brighter.

Clive nodded briefly at Emma and returned to his task. He was industriously stuffing tiny sacks into small cracks in the wooden wall of the prison.

Emma looked up and down the corridor, but she could not look far. The ceiling to her right had caved in, blocking the hallway completely. To her left, the passage was choked with dirt. Emma could see no sign of Sergeant Miller or his men, who had been just about to arrest every single one of them.

Savachia crouched by his father's limp body. He'd finagled his way into this prison, along with Emma, in order to rescue his father—but he hadn't told her about his plan. She had thought he'd been here to help her rescue Alex.

She'd been wrong. About that. About a lot of things.

Emma reached out to tug on Neil's soiled jacket. "There's no way out. We're buried alive!"

"Now, my dear, we are not buried. Although we are alive. Details count." Neil nodded at his flaming thumb. Emma's grip on his jacket threatened to pull his coat sleeve down over his hand, smothering the flame.

Emma quickly removed her hand.

"You have to have faith," said Neil. "Do you trust me?"

Emma hesitated.

No. The answer was no. She'd only just met the Grubian

brothers, shortly after flying skeletons called Rag-O-Rocs had invaded the mansion that belonged to Emma's uncle. Uncle Mordo had shouted at Emma and Alex to run, to save themselves, to follow Emma's pet rabbit, Pimawa. And they had.

Pimawa had turned out to be more than a pet. He was actually a Jimjarian, a walking, talking servant bound to serve a magician all his life. He'd brought them to the Conjurian, into the Mysts, where they were attacked by an entirely different kind of monster, a bandiloc. It had been Neil and Clive Grubian who'd saved them from the bandiloc and who'd taken Emma and Alex and Pimawa to Conjurian City.

Emma had thought they'd be safe there. That was one of the many things she'd been wrong about.

Conjurian City was where Emma had been kidnapped (by Savachia), where her brother Alex had been taken prisoner (by their uncle's old colleague Christopher Agglar), and where Emma had been told by the man who had been her dead parents' closest friend that he would not help her or protect her.

Conjurian City was where Emma had learned to trust no one at all.

But she had no choice now. She could not get herself out of this prison, where the collapsed roof and crushed walls and tons of dirt trapped her and the others more securely than locks and bars.

If Neil had a way out, she *had* to trust him.

She met his eyes and nodded.

Neil held the flame closer to Clive, who stuffed one last pouch into a small crevice and stepped back.

Emma had seen pouches like that before, in the Grubians' carriage. They had been full of woofle seeds. Emma didn't know much about woofle seeds, but she knew that they could explode.

Hope blossomed inside her, bright as Neil's flame. They weren't buried alive after all—or they wouldn't be for long!

Clive stepped back and spread his great arms, gesturing for all of them to step behind him. Emma did so quickly, nodding at Savachia to do the same. He was a liar and a traitor, and she would be sure to tell him exactly what she thought of him once they were free—but that didn't mean she wanted to see him blown up.

Savachia dragged his father behind Clive as the larger of the two Grubian brothers kicked the wall hard. Nothing happened.

"Kick harder, you elongated barber pole!" shouted Neil.

Clive kicked repeatedly.

"For the love of—move aside and let me—" Neil squirmed out from behind Clive just as the woofle seeds erupted in a blinding, golden flash. The tough wooden roots that made up the walls of the Conjurian Detention Center were wrenched apart, and the earth that surrounded them shuddered and split, revealing a slender fissure. Fresh air washed in.

"Ladies first." Neil coughed. He helped Emma into the crack. "When we get to the carriage," he added, jabbing a finger into his brother's gut, "you will spend the rest of the day checking the expiration dates on all the woofle seeds."

Emma clawed her way up, emerging into the giant field that lay at the foot of the Tower of Dedi. She looked around, hoping beyond hope to see Alex rushing toward her.

Instead she was enveloped in a curtain of sooty air. Chunks of wall and piles of brick and stone littered the plain and choked the gaps between the roots. She clambered up onto an arching root, desperately searching for the Tower of Dedi through the filthy air.

"Miss Emma!" croaked Neil, climbing out after her, followed by his brother. "We should stay low until the air clears." Rasping, Neil leaned against the root Emma was standing on. "Come down before someone, or something, spots you!"

A wind gust briefly cleared the murky sky, and Emma gasped. There, not more than two hundred yards away, stood what remained of the Tower of Dedi.

The last time Emma had been aboveground, the Tower had risen over this plain like a skyscraper. It was a building created out the largest living tree Emma had ever seen. It made a California redwood look like a spindly sapling.

And now it had fallen.

That was what had caused the cave-in, Emma realized. Not an earthquake. The Tower had collapsed.

Only the stump of the tree remained. The few surviving branches curled downward like the hands of a corpse.

"It's gone," said Emma.

Neil jerked his head up. Clive straightened up to stare. Savachia, tugging his father's body with him, was last to reach the surface. Even he seemed dumbstruck.

"My brother was in there," said Emma. "My brother was in the Tower!" She glared down at Savachia. "If you had done what you promised, he'd be alive!"

First Savachia had kidnapped Emma to use as a hostage. Then, after she'd begged and bargained, he'd agreed to help her sneak into the Tower to find Alex. But he hadn't done that. Instead he'd used her to get inside the Tower and then left her on her own while he went off to rescue his father.

Now, after one glance at the Tower, Savachia sat down in the dirt, bending over his father's motionless form.

"Now, now," said Neil, patting Emma's shoe. "I am sure a boy as clever as Alex found a way out. In fact, it is entirely possible he is responsible for the destruction we see before us. Probably took out Christopher Agglar and his henchmen in one go. The head of the Circle stood no chance against a boy as resourceful as your brother."

Emma stabbed her finger back toward the space where the Tower once stood. "No one got out of that! He's gone!" Her foot slipped.

Clive reached her in one stride. He wrapped his arms around her waist and lowered her gently to the ground.

Neil took her hand in his, patting it. "We made it out. Didn't we? And I daresay your brother is cleverer than the lot of us together."

Emma flung Neil's hand away, glaring down at Savachia. His back to her, he sat hunched over his father. It was as if he could not hear her.

Emma's fists were clenched so tightly that her fingernails cut into her palms. "This is your fault! I should never have trusted you!" she yelled at Savachia. "You're nothing more than a con artist! A no-good thief!"

Savachia shrugged. He got to his feet and walked a few steps away from his father, from Emma, from Neil and Clive. He stood with his back to them, looking at the devastation that surrounded them.

"Answer me!" Emma screamed at him.

He shrugged again, without turning.

"Ah, my dear Jane. Emma. Perhaps you might—" Neil ventured.

Emma ignored him. "What's the matter with you?" she demanded of Savachia.

"He's dead," Savachia said without looking at her.

Emma's breath and her words rushed out of her. She knew it. She knew Alex was gone. But to hear it like that, said so simply and brutally—it made her want to crumple to the ground.

Then she realized that Savachia was not talking about Alex at all.

Her eyes fell on the boy's father, lying faceup on the ground. The man didn't look much like Savachia at all. He was thin—well, he'd been in prison a long time. They didn't feed you all that well, probably. His hair and beard were disheveled. His eyes were closed, and his face was white. So white.

Of course, he'd been shut up in a cell away from the sun. Likely for a long time. But this kind of whiteness and stillness—Emma knew it could only mean one thing.

"Smothered, probably," said Savachia, still staring away. "Or a heart attack, maybe, when all that dirt came down over us. He wasn't strong. He'd been in that place so long."

Emma stared.

Her anger still sputtered and flared inside her, but how could she shriek at Savachia now? How could she batter at him with her fists or demand that he—what? Apologize? Fix what he'd done?

No apology could help. There was nothing to fix. Alex was dead. Just like Savachia's father was dead.

Neil cleared his throat.

"A tragedy indeed. My most sincere condolences. But now, my dears, we must figure out our next move."

Next move? A pain like no other, a hollow ache, filled Emma from head to toe. She had nothing left. No parents. No uncle. No brother. No home. She watched as Savachia pressed a kiss to his father's temple, then laid him on the dirt. What she was sure would be his final resting place.

Suddenly, Emma realized she had something after all, something new filling the void, replacing the ache: anger.

"I know what the next move is," said Emma. "I find the Shadow Conjurer and make him pay."

It was the Shadow Conjurer who'd sent the Rag-O-Rocs

to kill Uncle Mordo. It was the Shadow Conjurer who'd chased Emma and Alex into the Conjurian, a magical world where magic was slowly dying. It was the Shadow Conjurer's fault that Emma had lost everyone she'd ever loved.

"Well, okay, that was specific," said Neil, taken back. Suddenly he looked up at a shadow winding through the brackish sky toward them. "Rag-O-Roc! Run!"

"Let it come!" Emma shoved Clive aside and clambered back onto the root. Her teeth were clenched so tight she thought they might shatter. Her fists shook at her sides. The growing anger had given her power, and she liked it.

Clive attempted to bear-hug her legs. Emma hopped sideways out of his reach. No one was stopping her now! She wasn't going to run. Glowering at the beast on its collision course, she noticed something familiar. "It's not a Rag-O-Roc," she said, startled. "It's—"

The creature spiraled into Emma, sending them both crashing to the ground. "Geller!" Emma cradled the rumpled parrot. "What are you doing here?"

"I came to fetch my master after Master Agglar's thugs abducted him." Geller removed his cracked glasses, wiped them on his feathers, and balanced them back on his beak.

"Agglar's people took Derren?" Emma asked. She remembered how she'd last seen Derren Fallow—her parents' oldest friend—holding off Sergeant Miller, giving her time to flee with Savachia.

Derren had let her down. She'd gone to him for help, and he hadn't done a thing. But then he'd put himself at risk to let her escape.

So Derren had been arrested? Had he been inside the Tower too?

Geller flapped the dust from his wings. "Yes, indeed. But my master made it out. With the boy and the Jimjarian. I am afraid I lost them when the Tower fell."

Emma was glad she was already sitting on the ground, or she was sure she would have fallen over. *The boy.* Geller had said *the boy*. Did he mean . . . "Alex? Was Alex with Derren? And Pimawa? They're . . ." She had to stop to breathe. "Alive?"

"Certainly they were." Geller looked almost offended. "You don't think a trifle like a falling tower could have stopped my master, do you?"

Emma wanted to hug Geller—glasses, snooty look, and all. "Which way? Where were they headed?" she asked.

Geller scowled at her through the cracked lenses of his spectacles. "Toward the water."

Emma stood, placing Geller on a root. "Can you show us the way?" she asked eagerly.

Geller gingerly tested one wing. "It would appear I'm grounded for the time being. And it would take ages to climb though this debris."

"Well, taddely toophers, I'm not much of a climber," Neil said. He clapped his hands to his chest, choking on the grime that wafted from his jacket, and removed a small black box with a red button from an inside pocket. He pushed the button. A sharp double beep answered in the distance. "But I always have an escape plan from my escape plan."